ALL THE
TALES
WE TELL

This book is a work of fiction. Names, characters, places, and incidents are either products of the author's imagination or are used fictitiously. Any resemblance to actual persons, living or dead, business establishments, events, or locales is entirely coincidental. The author makes no claims to, but instead acknowledges the trademarked status and trademark owners of the wordmarks mentioned in this work of fiction including brands or products such as: Pepto Bismol, Range Rover, Barbie, Wikipedia, Laffy Taffy, Grey Goose, Big Bird and Swiffer.

ALL THE TALES WE TELL: Hearts Out of Water, Book 1
Copyright © 2013-2019 Annie Cosby.

Published by Snowy Wings Publishing.
www.snowywingspublishing.com

Cover designed by Regina Wamba of Mae I Design.
Interior by Key of Heart Designs.
Interior graphics designed by Dover Publications, Inc.

ISBN: 978-1-948661-23-2
eBook ISBN: 978-1-948661-22-5

Second Edition.

PRAISE FOR HEARTS OUT OF WATER

"A darkly romantic beginning to what promises to be an unusual
contemporary YA fantasy series."
- SERENA CHASE, *USA TODAY*

"A great mix of YA and Celtic Mythology."
- AMAZON REVIEWER

"This is such an enchanting story! Before reading this, I wasn't very
familiar with the Irish tales of selkies, but it was enthralling and
refreshing."
- AMAZON REVIEWER

ALL THE TALES WE TELL

HEARTS OUT OF WATER · BOOK ONE

ANNIE COSBY

FOR PRINCESS
who spent the entirety of this novel by my side

An Pálás Bándearg
THE PINK PALACE

OH MY," DAD SAID.

"This has to be a joke," I announced.

"It's perfect!" Mom clapped her hands happily.

We had just pulled up in front of that legendary house, the one we'd call ours this summer—and every summer thereafter if my mother had anything to do with it.

It was unmistakable, perched between two modestly whitewashed houses like a giant bottle of Pepto Bismol. An enormous block of solidified cotton candy. Now that my mother and her bleach-blonde hair had arrived, the place was only one plastic Ken doll short of a Barbie dreamhouse.

It even had a sign next to the front door with big, curly white letters against a purple background. The Pink Palace.

No shit.

I would have been cackling had the shock of my having to *sleep* here for the next three months not been too crippling.

Mom was already bouncing along toward the front door, babbling incessantly. I jogged to catch up as Dad went to begin unloading the trunk. Princess was already settling in, sniffing the bushes around the pink front steps.

We'd bought the house as-is. That meant that it was not fit to be lived in. So my father snapped it up "at a steal" and set his contractor friends to work on it. And then, when it was nearly finished, my mother set her decorators on it to make sure it would again not be fit to live in. At least not for anyone with a sensitive stomach.

"Cora! Your room's up here!"

I followed her voice up to the third floor, afraid of what I'd encounter. Surely a life-size Barbie or a shrine to kittens. Neither would have been out of place. Mom's team had wholeheartedly seized the house's century-old name.

"It's a girl," I said lamely, entering what would apparently be "my room."

It was big, with a king-size bed in the middle and a full-length mirror and a dresser on either side. But it was pink. There was a cool trunk at the foot of the bed that was the natural brown of wood, but everything else in the room, from the curtains to the mismatched lamps that sat around the room on various pieces of furniture, would rival the pink of any baby's butt.

"Isn't it delightful?" Mom screeched.

It had a big balcony that looked out onto the beach, which was promising, but I couldn't take her happiness right now. Nothing would make her think badly of this house and this summer she had been so long in preparing. Not even my loudest whining or most stinging sarcasm. As if I wanted to be *here*, hundreds of miles from home, during my last summer before my high school friends disappeared from my life.

"It's lovely, Mom." I tried to keep my voice monotone. "It's all just *too* lovely." I turned around and tramped back down the pink-carpeted stairs.

"Where are you going?" Mom demanded, skipping down the stairs after me.

The front door lay open and I could see the Range Rover outside, trunk open, and suitcases spilling out. Dad was near snoring on the couch. I pushed through a swinging door into the kitchen, which, surrounding a matching tiled floor, countertops and painted cabinets, was a hazy cloud of puce.

"I'm just going out."

"What do you mean 'out'? You don't know a soul here!" When it was clear I wasn't going to respond, Mom went on. "Make sure you're back by five, we need to get you cleaned up for the barbecue."

"The *what*?" I swirled around abruptly.

Mom rolled her eyes and heaved a dramatic sigh. "Honestly, Cora, do you ever listen? The barbecue the Carltons invited us to. I've told you about it a million times. It's to kick off the season and celebrate the holiday weekend. Everyone's going to be there!"

"Who are the Carltons? And who's 'everyone'?" That *definitely* did not include me. I was too awkward a person to enjoy introductions and small talk.

"Oh, Linda Carlton is just divine! The realtor gave us her number. A must-know in this neighborhood. And she has a son your age who sounds just *charming!*"

I intended to groan inwardly, but it must have been audible, because Mom's face darkened.

"Oh, you *will* go, and you will have the time of your life!" It was a demand, as if she could make me feel good or bad at her will. "And you will be an absolute *doll* to this Owen Carlton! He just graduated, too, and he likes to boat and play water polo. And above it all, he has his own sailboat! Oh, how I wished we lived on the coast and you could have a sailboat, Cora."

"Eh, I'm good."

"Oh, and this Owen, I think he's going to an Ivy—"

Nope. I was not going to talk about that. Not now. "I'm going out," I said decisively.

I headed for the back door, which was, miraculously, an off-white color. Oh, wonderful haven to my eyes! I grabbed the brass handle—

"Unlike that Josh Watson."

My heart stopped. I turned slowly around.

"Where's he going? Stanford?" She wrinkled her nose as if Stanford were a pile of rubbish and not a fantastic university.

He's not going to Stanford, I thought miserably. Those shiny blue eyes were going to *Western.*

"This Owen—"

"Are you *seriously* bringing this up right now? Mom—"

"Actually, on second thought, I'm fairly sure the Watsons hold some sway at Stanford. Maybe we could email them—"

"*What?* No!"

It was quickly becoming clear to me. She saw this summer away as some kind of fix-all. Some kind of cure for every problem she'd ever had. Especially concerning me. This summer was supposed to fix *me*.

"We'll talk about it later," she said, becoming interested in the arrangement of the kitchen table and chairs. "Oh, and do be careful," she added. "Linda tells me there's a sordid crowd that runs around here, too. Petty robberies and things of that sort. Not ideal for a summer away, but … And don't forget we need to go up to the pool and sign up for swimming lessons!"

My stomach dropped to the pink tiled floor and my will to fight left me. She did, indeed, have a whole plan to fix me. I pushed open the back door and dashed through before letting it slam on whatever afterthought was currently leaving my mother's mouth.

A wide set of stairs led from the back porch across the backyard. Low and long, they ended in a curving flourish at the public boardwalk that ran horizontal along the beach. I wandered aimlessly down the boardwalk and it wasn't long before I lost sight of the Pink Atrocity.

Out of sight, out of mind, I sighed.

I found myself in the middle of a great expanse of tiny red wooden cabins with a few mismatched houses interspersed. I was decidedly outside my comfort zone, but I couldn't figure out how to get back to the row of old houses in the distance.

It's like a frickin' standardized test, I thought glumly. I'd always done badly on the maps portion.

At one particular fork in the boardwalk, I chose left at random— hoping it would lead to the pink monstrosity in the distance.

I realized my mistake too late. The boardwalk snaked toward the biggest of the dodgy red cabins, a two-story deal with chipping paint and the word "office" painted in a window. A sign swung in the breeze above the door. It said "O'Brien Resort" and creaked like a verbal warning of imminent danger. I wondered vaguely if there was a seaside motel in the *Saw* movies …

"Are you lost, dear?"

I nearly jumped out of my skin. I whirled frantically about to find the source of the voice.

A tiny old woman sat on the porch of a house a few yards back from the boardwalk. I'd taken no notice of the small yellow house when passing by, as most of the houses this way were just as tumbled down as the red cabins around them.

The yellow house was short and squat, the paint faded and chipping around the windows. A round window peeked from above the porch but it was dark and cloudy.

"I'm sorry," the old woman said. She talked so slowly it sounded like she might kick the bucket any minute now. "Did I scare you?"

Yes, I find you incredibly freaky, I thought. *Your little house is creepy and your voice is like bugs crawling on my skin.* "No," I chirped aloud.

"The ocean *can* make one jumpy," she smiled.

You have no *idea.*

One of her wrinkled hands strayed to absently touch the shiny paisley scarf covering her hair. "Do you need directions somewhere?" The hand wandered down her short neck and finally settled back in her lap.

"No," I stammered, "I'm just looking." *Just looking?* For what? An early death?

"Oh, yes, there is a lot to look at, isn't there?" The old woman seemed pleased with this. She sat in a huge wooden rocking chair, bobbing slowly but diligently back and forth. It creaked—either the chair or the woman's old joints—at regular intervals. A matching chair rocked, empty beside her. An effect of the wind rolling off the ocean, no doubt, but a shiver skittered down my spine nonetheless.

"The best suns are always after the best storms," she said.

I nodded, though she didn't look at me. Her dark eyes, after appraising me once, had returned to roving the horizon of the ocean, never stopping to linger over anything in particular. Her hands lay limply in her lap as her feet, in house slippers, kept the chair rocking.

"The waves are big today," she continued. "There was a puddle over there, thought maybe the sun had caught an ashray."

My automatic grunt of a response died in my throat. *Ash* what?

"Nothing left but a puddle of water if it's caught in the sun. They're nocturnal, you know." She looked at me this time.

"I … uh, yeah …" *No,* no, I didn't know, and I sure as hell didn't *want* to know.

"So you must never swim at night. But do watch for water spirits," she said. "Not all dangers are nocturnal."

"Water spirits. Of course." I nodded vaguely because asking what a water spirit was would be counterproductive to my escaping this terrifying conversation.

"You'll help me, won't you, dear?" she said, without looking at me.

"I ..." *have absolutely no response for this.* What on earth could I help her with?

"And make sure you are careful, when you go to swim."

I grabbed at the excuse. "Yes, of course, and—and I was just on my way to do that—to go swim—I should be going. Swimming. That way." I backed away slowly, waiting for her to toss another warning about ashbugs at me, but she was only nodding slowly at the horizon.

As if I needed more reasons to be terrified of the water—water ghosts hadn't even made my preexisting list. Summer in this town was going to be worse than I'd previously assumed. Already 100 percent of the population I'd met was certifiably whacko.

She didn't seem to notice I was slipping away, so I whipped around and hurried back in the direction from which I'd come. At that fateful, unfortunate fork, I took the other option and was quickly delivered to the grassy patch behind the pink house.

A night of small talk with women like my mother, and even that sure-to-be odious Owen Carlton, would be a piece of cake after the conversation I'd just had.

An Rogha Deirneach
THE LAST RESORT

THAT EVENING, I EMERGED FROM MY NEW ROOM in a lacey cream dress. I'd first appeared in my jeans and a t-shirt from school, but I'd been quickly sent back to retry—this time with directions.

"There; isn't that better?" Mom watched me swish grumpily down the stairs.

"She looks great," Dad said, even though his nose was buried in a newspaper and not paying the least bit of attention to what I was wearing.

"Oh, Cora, flip-flops?" Mom wailed. "Where are those adorable purple wedges I found for you in New York?"

"I left them at home." My best friend Rosie had insisted I pack them after deeming them "the cutest thing ever." But she had ditched me shortly thereafter to be with her boyfriend and I had stowed the shoes away under my bed for the summer—and forever thereafter if I had a say in it.

"Oh, *Cora!*" she wailed. "Regardless, I want you to make a just *lovely* impression on Owen Carlton—"

"Yes, your mom is just short of arranging your marriage," Dad cut in. "So you'd better make such an impression tonight that this Carlton woman and her son will want nothing to do with you in the future."

"Oh, Frank!" Mom exclaimed happily. "Why do you encourage her?"

"She looks like an angel—let's go," Dad said decisively. He folded his newspaper shut, laid it on the table, and headed for the back door.

I followed with a scowl. The last thing I wanted to do right now was feign interest in small talk, introductions, and *especially* snotty boys.

From the back stairs you could see most of Oyster Beach. To the north stood big, old houses like ours (though less ostentatiously painted) that sat far back from the beach in a proud line. Smaller paths and stairs like ours lead across huge sandy backyards and screened-in porches.

It was toward this backyard, summer bliss that we turned now. But behind us, the south of Oyster Beach looked like a wilderness from our porch. A messy tangle of boardwalk threading through that eerie jumble of deep-red cabins. I looked for the creepy old woman's yellow house, but I couldn't pick it out in the time before my mom shouted for me to catch up.

The barbecue was in the backyard of a huge three-story deal about ten houses down from ours. It belonged to a family called Ritz, and it apparently wasn't the biggest of the bunch, according to the blasé way in which everyone referenced it.

A Mrs. Huston, who had called me "the nicest little darling," even hinted that Ritz Manor was quickly being outgrown by the Ritz family. Six bedrooms weren't quite sufficient.

"How many children are there?" Mom was in her element here. She wore a pale lavender-colored pant suit with billowing legs that whipped softly at her ankles. She brandished a big glass of wine like it was part of her outfit.

"The Ritzes have two."

I was glued to my mom's side—and, thus, Mrs. Huston's. Dad was playing washers with some men whose shouts were becoming increasingly boisterous as they made their way through the beer on tap in the pool house.

"Cora, you must meet my Benjamin," Mrs. Huston was saying. She twirled around looking for her son, some of her margarita slopping over the edge of her glass as she spotted him. She called him over the sloping lawn before I could protest.

Several of his peers followed him from their mob beside the giant pool (that looked more like a pond) to have a gawk at me, as if some big, exotic bird had just landed inexplicably beside the house.

And much to my chagrin, I was promptly deserted by my mother. She insisted on a full tour of the Ritzes' extensive lawn ornament collection, and Mrs. Huston was only too willing to expound on her knowledge of it all. My feeble protests were ignored, and I was left with a wink to fend for myself in this overwhelming world of bare, tanned shoulders and the smell of salt.

The necessary introductions already having passed, the Huston boy stood awkwardly a few feet from me, his friends obviously giving me the once- and twice- and, by this time, thrice-over.

"So you're from Missouri?" a blonde girl asked suddenly.

"Yeah, yeah," I said lamely. "St. Louis." I felt the need to clarify. Some of these kids spoke with distinct New England vowels and a few even had lazy Southern drawls, but their clothes were pressed and distressed to perfection, their hair dyed, teased and cut in ways I'd only seen in magazines.

"Why are you *here*? Isn't that like, really far away?"

I was seriously going to slap this blonde girl.

"Yeah, where is Missouri?" another girl piped up. She was dressed in shorts entirely too short for human legs and a tank top entirely too tight for human torsos. "I don't even know where it is." She snorted derisively, as if this somehow proved my inconsequentiality instead of her ignorance.

"It's between Kansas and Illinois ..." I faltered at the blank stares I received. "Near Chicago." That was a stretch.

"*Ohhh!*"

There was no need to explain the three hundred miles between the two cities, as the majority of the kids had already wandered away in boredom—with the realization that the new bird wasn't quite as exotic as they had hoped. Even the Huston kid had hightailed it without so much as a nice-to-meet-you.

The only ones left standing before my anxious eyes were Blondie, the bimbo and a boy who smirked at me, but stood like an

Abercrombie model with his hands perched on his hips.

"So why *are* you here?" Blondie asked.

"Lay off her," the Abercrombie model piped up.

"What?" Blondie exuded innocence. "I'm just asking."

"My parents just bought a house," I explained.

"Which house?"

My cheeks flared to match the words I was about to speak. "The Pink Palace."

Blondie chuckled. The bimbo flicked her head to shake her bangs out of her eyes. "That's been deserted forever."

If I'd had any say, it would have stayed that way.

"I hope you have plans to repaint," Abercrombie said. I glared at him, but his smile was playful, not provoking.

"It must've been really cheap," Blondie cut in. "Like, a real fixer-upper."

I shrugged noncommittally.

"It's just weird to have someone new here," Blondie went on. "We don't really get new people." She flicked her head in an exact imitation of her friend. Her blonde bangs whipped around and landed perfectly across her forehead. "These are all, like, real old families that have been summering here forever. We've all been neighbors since we were, like, born."

I don't want to be here, like, *any more than you want me here, you infuriating dimwit.*

"We don't see a whole lot of people from Missouri." The bimbo, though just as annoying, didn't have the same vitriol in her voice that Blondie did. She just seemed … well, clueless.

"People at home just don't really think much of coming *here*, of all places," I said.

"Why?"

Damn ... that had been a complete lie. My friends thought it was über cool that I got to "summer" away from home. Time for my finest bullshitting.

"I guess there's just not, like, a lot of people in Missouri who can afford summer houses," the bimbo answered for me. She seemed to regard this as some critical shortfall of Missourians.

"Most people's summer houses are on the lake," I corrected, gathering steam from my anger. "You know, on the lake there's a ton of skiing and night life and stuff. Usually the only people who come out here are, like, old people." I hated myself as I groped for approval from these kids, but I also couldn't stop. "I tried to convince my parents to get a house on the lake instead, but, you know parents. Really boring. Wanted to come out here."

Abercrombie took a step forward. "It's a shame you had to be banished to the ends of the earth with the rest of us."

Blondie feigned a smirk, but it turned out more like a grimace.

Afraid of what else I'd lie about if left to my own embarrassed, wandering mouth, I excused myself on the grounds of needing to use the restroom. The Abercrombie model grinned stupidly at me as I hightailed it.

I told my dad I wasn't feeling well and skipped out of the waist-high white gate that enclosed the elite gathering. I congratulated myself on escaping the premarital introduction that my mother was undoubtedly trying to arrange with the famous Owen Carlton that very moment.

But if I was being truthful with myself (which I wasn't), I was a little lonely, too. I took my shoes off and walked in the sandy grass beside the boardwalk, the sun casting an orange glow over it all.

Everything was just sand—it seemed to consume everything. It covered the landscape, as if smothering anything that tried to push out of the ground. Definitely a place where water spirits and ashrays— whatever they were—could thrive. And now, in the strong wind that hinted of a storm, the feeble grass whipped mercilessly at my legs.

Suddenly my big toe caught on something hard and cold, and I jumped.

Get a grip!

I reached down to pry the thing from where it was lodged in the sand. To my relief, it was just some sort of musical instrument. I brushed it off with my dress; it was long and silver with six round holes. It looked like a small flute.

My first instinct was to blow into it, see the sound it would make, get the sand out, but I was too wary of its previous owners. And I was reminded of the disgusted way in which I'd heard the word "locals" pronounced by numerous people in the old houses.

I was also afraid to draw attention to myself from the crowd of families that still laughed and played in the yard behind me. I gave the hubbub one more glance over my shoulder before dropping the flute into one of the big pockets on the front of my dress and moving off with a renewed desire to get away from the Ritz estate.

The Pink Palace was silent. I meant to relish the quiet in my room, but as I moved through the kitchen, an envelope on the table caught my eye.

There was a messy pile of mail there, obviously left to be read later, but one was addressed to me in our housekeeper's curly handwriting. Deep in her seventies, Joan avoided computers and so it wasn't unusual for me to get letters from her while we were away. But we'd left less than forty-eight hours ago and this particular envelope bore a same-day delivery stamp.

I ripped it open. Inside was another envelope, this one with a post-it stuck to the front. A note from Joan.

"Honey, this came for you just after you left. Made sure to camouflage it so you could read it first. Love, Joan."

A smile crept onto my face. She knew my mother too well. Mom would assume that any important mail addressed to me was surely also meant for the woman who had spawned me eighteen years ago.

I crumpled up the post-it, lest my mother should find it, and looked at the hidden envelope. The return address was the admissions office at Western University.

And there, I faltered. My hands trembled. My fingers left little sweat fingerprints on the envelope. How long did I stand there, contemplating the feel of the paper beneath my fingers?

The envelope was still sealed. Joan hadn't read it. I could let everyone believe I'd been rejected and run away to Europe. Or to California. Or Mexico. Or New York City. The simple act of running away was something I ached to do with every fiber of my being. End the struggle that was school and tests and studying. Find something else to define me. My thumb brushed across my name printed on the envelope.

Cora Manchester.

It was no use. Inside me, deeper than the desire to run away, was a little part of me that wanted to be accepted, too. Needed to be accepted. For my own self-respect.

I took a deep breath and ripped the envelope open; I unfolded it with shaking fingers.

"I regret to inform you …"

My stomach slid to my feet. Apparently that form dismissal wasn't an urban legend. Those words did exist in real life. And they hurt more than any book or movie could portray.

I stopped reading. I didn't need to read that my GPA had been too low. That other kids were smarter than me. More talented than me. Could play basketball or softball without tripping.

The threat of tears stung my eyes. *Why does this hurt so much?* I hadn't even thought I cared! I was furious with myself. Had I been harboring this secret fantasy of going to Western all along? Going to the school my parents wanted me to go to, going to school with Josh Watson and lusting after him for another four years? Or was I just afraid of the looks I would get when my parents found out?

The last thing I wanted was to be caught crying by my parents. It was a habit very much abhorred by my father. I crumpled the letter and threw it in the trash. Then I pulled on a sweatshirt and left.

I needed to put as much space as possible between me and that horrible letter, those hurtful words and that shockingly pink house.

I walked quickly, without much care for where I wandered, and I soon found myself amid that mess of red cabins again.

The cabins were all uniformly painted—red with white trim—and seemed to be chipping and fading in unison. People buzzed in and out of the little cabins. Several fathers bearing beer and mothers with children in tow swirled around me.

My eyes stinging with those unwanted tears, I nearly bounced into an old man with a metal detector. He gave me a scornful look, but I quickly lowered my gaze and strode on.

Eventually the activity and cabins died away, too, and I came to an unkempt area of beach with seaweed strewn about. There were no people here, and behind the beach the dunes had given way to rocky hills.

Just a little farther on, I spotted a tiny run-down pier. It was a short wooden thing raised on piles, with a wide walkway of wooden slats. But it also looked old, the dark piles rising along the sides like crooked teeth. It extended into the ocean a few yards, the end sloping and shifting ominously in the waves.

I sat down in the sand before the pier, tired of walking but not courageous enough to test the strength of the pier itself, and wrapped my arms around my legs. The angry ocean waves roiled and crashed into each other, spraying my face with cold droplets. And here, quite alone, I dared to cry.

The tears came in a torrent. The last two days had been the longest of my life, cramped in the back of the car with three months' worth of junk and a worrisome dog that thought every car ride ended at the vet. My mind had been boiling with the last year's buildup of thoughts as we stopped at antique store after tiny store along the highway. But here on the beach, I felt far away from everything I'd left at home. The best friend. The best friend's new boyfriend. The almost-but-never-was-mine boy friend. Not to mention school.

It had all felt so far away for a few hours. But that letter had followed me. That was it—my one reserve. *Gone.* Still, that familiar feeling of waiting wasn't gone yet. That vague but completely familiar feeling followed me all the way to this beach, so far away from my blue room in the suburban house where I cried myself to sleep when I got wait-listed at every private college in the Midwest and when Josh Watson declared he didn't like me and where I sat alone weekends when Rosie went out with Steve.

And just when I had managed to sort through all that, I saw it. Something in the water.

My thoughts raced immediately to ashrays. In my mind, they were big blue things that resembled sharks. But this seemed too round to be anything menacing, perhaps a sea lion. I got up to take a few steps closer and squinted my eyes. And then a wave pushed the head above water, and it became clear that the creature wasn't a seal at all.

It was a person. A very wet, very puffy person.

I screamed.

Ag Troid le Anam an Gheimhridh
BATTLING THE SPIRIT OF WINTER

THE NEXT MORNING I WOKE UP WHEN THE HOUSE was still silent. It had stormed as soon as we'd gotten home, but the storm had died in the night. It wasn't usual that I woke up before my parents, or even before noon. But last night had been one unlike any other, and I couldn't fall back asleep. So I slipped into my flip-flops and thwapped out to the back porch.

Princess followed me as I marched off, confident I could find my way back to the pier.

But when it came into sight, it was empty. I don't know what I was expecting. Perhaps a few lingering gawkers, maybe some police tape. But the local police chief, Captain Harville, had called just around midnight to tell my mom that everything was wrapped up—the body belonged to a man who lived a few miles south of the city—and to make sure I was okay.

I had insisted I was fine, the old man with the metal detector had arrived quickly and ushered me away too fast for any lasting mental images. It had all ended so quickly. It was … anticlimactic. I couldn't believe I was saying it, but there it was. Finding a dead body hadn't been nearly as exciting as one would think.

It wasn't a horror movie. The dead man had been a sailor. A ship had gone done a few towns over and several men had disappeared; not all the bodies had been accounted for yet. It was unusual for a body to drift this far, they said. They hadn't been searching so far north. But because of the tides, they could continue searching for weeks.

A very cut-and-dry event for me. It had all been cleaned up nicely, as horrendous as it had started out. Still, I was curious.

But the pier was empty.

And in the bright sun and calm waves of the early morning, it definitely didn't look the stuff of horror movies. Princess pranced happily to the end of the pier and back. For all its looks, it could have been the site of a children's swimming lesson. *A swimming lesson.*

A chill ran through my body involuntarily.

You're insane, I thought. *Dead body, no sweat. But swimming lessons? The stuff of nightmares.*

My inner conversation died away as I slowly became aware of a figure in the water a few yards out. And this was not a dead body. This was a very alive person. A young man.

I watched curiously as the boy swam, his dark head ducking under the water every so often as he stroked. The water made his tan skin shine brilliantly. It was unusual to see someone swimming so diligently along in the ocean. I'd always associated the beach with kids splashing and teenage girls giggling in bikini tops. And of course, now, dead bodies, too. I wondered if that boy knew what had been in that water just last night.

Princess whined at me and I shushed her so as not to draw attention from the swimmer. I was mesmerized, watching him as his rigid arms sliced through the waves. In the distance, he stopped to rub his eyes and shake his head like a wet dog before starting up again.

It was like magic to me. The way he flew through the waves, bobbing with them, but stronger than them. So opposite of that bloated body with the soggy clothes. I had imagined glimpsing a pale face, but in retrospect, I knew my imagination had created it. The body had been too far out to make out its features.

In the distance, the living boy reversed direction and came back toward us. I snapped myself out of whatever reverie was coming, and pulled Princess back to the beach.

I didn't want to disturb the seriousness about the ocean at this time of morning—or explain to a stranger why I was watching him swim. That was stalker material.

"Are you lost?"

I was. But I was also not going to admit it.

"No, just looking."

"Really? Because you look really lost."

I managed a small, fake laugh and twirled around. "Well, yeah, I was trying to find Main Street. The map said it went right up to a dead end near O'Brien Resort."

The girl with the blond pigtails nodded. I noticed her eyes were puffy and red, as though she had been crying. "Yeah, you just passed it. It's right back there." She jabbed a thumb over her shoulder in the direction I'd come.

I mumbled an embarrassed thanks and moved to go back the way I'd come, but she unconsciously blocked the boardwalk.

"Are you staying in the resort?" she asked. She said it placidly enough, but she was one of those tall, leggy blondes that made me feel inferior in every possible way.

I shook my head. "My parents have a house back down there." I waved vaguely, and the girl's eyes narrowed infinitesimally. Her lips were a tight round O. Her red eyes flew over me once before she sniffed, nodded and walked on. "Cool." It was a mutter meant only for pretension; I could hear the judgment behind it.

And then I recognized where I was. Somehow I'd managed to find myself back near that old woman's dumpy house!

Of course she was sitting in the rocker, her dark hands a bundle in her lap. And of course she recognized me immediately.

"Hello, are you lost?"

Or didn't recognize me, for that matter.

"No," I said. "I'm just—going that way." *Note to self: Practice excuses!*

"It's nice weather today, isn't it?" the little old woman said.

I didn't want to get roped back into her suffocating conversation but I had no way out.

"Do come sit with me, dear. It's such a nice day." Her eyes flickered from the ocean to me and back to the water as she patted the empty rocking chair next to her. That damned creepy rocking chair that rocked itself to the beat of the ocean waves.

I stalled, looking around for inspiration for a polite refusal.

She patted the rocking chair again, her eyes still staring out at the ocean with a frightful intensity, almost as though blind, as though she was unable to focus her eyes on me. "Sit, sit. It's hot out there, and I'm old and lonely." She spoke slowly, giving authenticity to her claims.

"Well, I have to take my dog to … um …" *Shit.*

"Oh, I do love a kindred soul," the old woman's eyes lit up and left the ocean long enough to flit to Princess, who stood confused at my feet. She wanted clearance to go and greet the new human friend. "Please." The old woman patted the rocking chair and clapped her hands absently. Princess looked up at me eagerly, asking my permission to give in to the excitement of the clapping.

I sighed and resignedly climbed the stairs. Princess took off to sniff the old woman who finally pulled her eyes from the ocean to laugh and pet the Beagle. "What a dear creature. What's his name?"

"Princess," I said.

"Oh, I'm sorry, miss." She was speaking to Princess, but she tapped the rocking chair beside her one last time.

I gave in and sat awkwardly on the edge of the chair as Princess settled at the old woman's feet, her tail going a thousand miles per hour.

"And what's your name, dear?"

"Cora."

"Oh, how pretty." The conversation was languid and rolled along slowly with her moderate speech. Almost to the tempo of the waves. It gave the impression that she weighed and considered each word carefully. This was a skill unknown to me. "And do you live near here, Cora?"

"For the summer," I said.

"How nice." Her eyes were back on the ocean, one hand limp in her lap, the other stroking Princess's ears. Her little feet were firmly planted on the floor, keeping the chair rocking at a steady, slow pace to match her slow words. Her incessant bobbing back and forth and her distant eyes gave her the air of a rather insane person. The kind you saw tied up in straight jackets in insane asylums in old movies. I shifted uncomfortably in my chair.

"Do you like the sea?" she asked me.

I nodded.

"You can't get better weather than this, yes?"

I nodded again and, starting to feel like a mute, racked my brain for some way to contribute to the conversation. "And it was really stormy just a few days ago," I said lamely.

The old woman nodded knowingly. "And that's precisely how it goes. The storms in the spring giving way to the summer calm. You know, of course, the cycle of the sea?"

Without her eyes leaving the ocean, she seemed to know I'd shaken my head.

"Those storms in the spring, always in the spring, it's the Sea Mother battling against the spirit of winter. The spirit of winter, they call him here, some call him Teran. And he battles the Sea Mother in the spring."

I stared at her plainly, but she was engrossed in the ocean and her story, her big round eyes trolling the horizon.

"And the Sea Mother is victorious and banishes him to the bottom of the sea for the summer. And Teran sometimes causes a squall here and there as he tries to break free. But they say he won't get free. Not until the autumn when he and the Sea Mother battle again. And that time, Teran will win. And then he will lord over the sea until they battle again in the spring. And it is an endless cycle, just like the sea itself."

When she finished, her eyes flitted to my face and I looked away hurriedly, not wanting to be caught staring.

"You are skeptical, like my Seamus was in the beginning," she said.

I opened my mouth to politely protest, but nothing came out. *Skeptical* wasn't strong enough a word.

Something seemed to occur suddenly to the old woman. "Dear," she said, "would you fetch me my coat?" She didn't even look at me. "It's just inside."

With the rest of the bodies, no doubt.

She sensed my hesitation. "Just inside the door there. Be a dear."

You've got to be kidding me! It was at least eighty-five degrees in the summer air.

She nodded encouragingly toward the door.

I got up a little nervously, and peered through the screen door. The inner door was open, giving way to a dim interior. I wanted to protest, to run away in fear, but the old woman looked so tiny and helpless, hunched over in her rocking chair. There was something lonely about her. Almost pathetic. The image of the pale, bloated body from last night floated through my mind, but I pushed it quickly away.

The wooden screen door creaked as I opened it, bracing myself for some sort of shrine to the Sea Mother or ashrays. "Where is it?" I called, as the door shut noisily behind me.

"I haven't seen it in ages, dear," she called back.

Well then I'll surely be able to find it.

The room I was standing in was dark and musty. I could see tiny particles of dust sailing through the shafts of light that illuminated the old carpet. The room was crowded with sofas and plush chairs, but it was tidy—no jacket thrown across the back of any furniture. It was not clean, exactly, but had more the air of something not having been touched in a very long time. The walls were covered with shelves laden with books of every size and color. The spines made a kind of dark rainbow across the walls, and there were seashells everywhere. I mean *everywhere.* They were on the tops of books, tables, the floor, and even one of the sofas.

There was a narrow archway in the back of the room that led to a room even darker than this one, but after examining a few of the nearest books (*A History of Berlin* and *Nymphs: A Complete Guide*), I figured I could pretend I'd spent my requisite time searching.

"I couldn't find it," I said, emerging back onto the porch where the light was slowly softening as the sun began to fall.

"Yes, thank you for looking," the old woman said with a pleasant, though disappointed, smile.

"Are you cold? It's warm inside," I said.

"No, no, not at all, please come sit. I get quite lonely with Ronan the only one who comes to call. Come, tell me what brings you to the ocean if you are quite decided against believing her."

I slid back onto the empty rocking chair. "My parents brought us here for the summer," I said.

"They made you come, then." It wasn't a question, but a statement. "You are a young lady, you think your life is full, and parents don't always fit into that life. Are you an only child, my dear?"

"Yes," I said. *Creepy, or a lucky guess?* I couldn't decide.

She was nodding slowly now. "Tell me, dear, what is it that divides you from your parents?"

"I don't know, my mom just …" I thought for a moment, trying to pin my discontent on a single thing. "I just graduated from high school," I said weakly.

"Ah," she nodded again in that slow, knowing way. "You have grown right out of your childhood and they are not ready for that."

"We just can't agree on what I'm going to do next year," I said.

"Ah," she said again. "And what is it they want you to do?"

"Go to college."

She was quiet for a moment, still swaying in the rocking chair. "And this is such a terrible fate?"

I would look back on this moment and wonder what had brought me to indulge this old woman's questions. But at the time, it felt natural to tell her these things.

"I just didn't get into the school I wanted," I said. *Or any of them.* I paused. "And I'd rather take a year off." She was quiet again, and I read her disapproval in the silence. "To travel," I added, trying to justify it. "See the world before I condemn myself to a degree and a career."

"And your parents will not allow this."

"We always argue about it."

"Your mother does not want that path for you. As mine did not want for me."

I was surprised. "You skipped a year before college?"

The woman laughed a dry, brittle, almost sad laugh. "I wanted to see the world and my mother did not want it for me. It is dangerous."

"She thinks I won't go to college if I skip a year," I said. "But it would only be a year, I *want* to go to college." *But on* my *terms.* I didn't want to be the dumb girl the college let in because her dad knew the dean. "I'm not ready. Just not right now."

"Time has a way of binding us. Months turn into years against our will."

I was silent.

"I never returned to my mother," the old woman said, and I saw her eyes narrow almost imperceptibly as they swept the horizon.

"I'm sorry," I said lamely.

We were both quiet for a few minutes, and the noise of the ocean seemed to heighten to a roar in the silence. I began to feel awkward and tried to make my escape. "I really should get going," I said, standing up. "It was really nice meeting you."

"Cora, that is not to say I would not do it again, had I the chance." I froze, standing awkwardly near the stairs. "Yes, I would *always* go again," she said.

"I'm glad," I murmured. And I was. To know the adventure might be worth it, whatever the adventure might be.

The old woman was nodding, her hands back in her lap. "At the end, the pros will always outweigh the cons, and so you must do what *you* feel you need. In your heart."

Now I was the one nodding in her strange, slow fashion.

"And Cora?" She was smiling faintly. "It *is* dangerous."

Ar Mhaithe le Honóir
KEEPING UP APPEARANCES

HE SUN WAS JUST SETTLING OVER THE BACKS OF the sprawling yards of the old houses as I jogged home. I'd forgotten my phone at the Pink Palace (on purpose), and it was after dinnertime. A tongue-lashing was in my immediate future.

I ran up the back stairs prepared for the combined anger of my parents, but somewhat emboldened by the old woman's words. The adventure was always worth it.

It occurred to me that I hadn't even asked her name. She had gone on about mine and even Princess's, and I hadn't even considered hers. But her message had reached me loud and clear. I had every intention of going into that house and revealing that Western had, indeed, rejected me and so I was not going to college in the fall.

But when I burst through the back door, I stopped

dead in my tracks. Princess ran in ahead of me and scurried around the dining room table excitedly. It was set for dinner as I had expected, but it was also surrounded by people.

"Cora, we've been worried sick about you," Mom said with a beaming smile that belied her true feelings.

The meal was in full swing, but everyone had politely stopped eating to watch me stumble awkwardly into the room. *Wonderful. An audience for my declaration of independence.*

"We thought you'd fallen in," a strange woman said genially.

I cringed and hazarded a look at my mother, who had a stiff smile plastered to her face.

Dad cleared his throat, bringing my mother back to the present. "Saved you some lobster, Cora," he said. He was the first to return to said lobster. The man sitting next to him followed suit, then the woman who had spoken, and what appeared to be their daughter. And, lastly, my eyes fell to the young man brandishing his lobster with a popped collar and a smirk. Mr. Abercrombie.

"Come sit down and meet the Carltons, honey." My mother was all blinding, bleached teeth and smiles.

I sat down awkwardly in the only empty chair left, across from the Carlton boy. Undoubtedly a strategic move by my mother. She chirped introductions as she shoveled all sorts of food onto my plate. "And, of course, this is Owen."

Abercrombie smiled at me. "Hi, Cora." His voice was deeper than I remembered.

"Dear, I heard you were involved in some strange happenings

down south," Mrs. Carlton said to me, her face quite alarmed. She was a pointy-faced woman with eyebrows too high to be natural.

I looked to my mother for guidance. She was wearing a similarly tragic expression. "Not really," I said. "I just happened to be there."

"Yes, how true," Mrs. Carlton said.

"Yes, it all happened so fast, Cora hardly saw a thing," Mom said with a polite smile. "No lasting damage done."

Not that you asked. In fact, the topic hadn't been broached at all once we'd left the police at the pier. *Best to brush unpleasant things under expensive rugs.*

"Well," Mrs. Carlton went on. "That just goes to show how you children should stay away from that area. A rough place. Best to stay among the old houses." She placed a protective hand on her own daughter's shoulder. The girl was a pudgy little replica of her mother. But she had yet to stop sucking food into her mouth long enough to speak.

"Yes, Cora has certainly learned her lesson, no more hanging around down there," my mother said, before moving on to a topic more pleasing to her (antique deck furniture).

I glanced at Abercrombie to see if he was buying this blame-the-south skit, but he wasn't paying attention, just pushing vegetables around his plate absently. Every so often he shot a glance at me, smirking when he caught my eye. Or maybe it was all in my head. He was cute enough, "hotter than a Brad Pitt knockoff" being Rosie's phrase of the month. But his shaggy bleach-blond hair was shinier than that of most girls I knew, and his demeanor suggested a teenage boy who knows *exactly* how attractive he is.

I despised this.

His mother's high-pitched drawl interrupted my thoughts when I heard my name.

Huh?

"Cora is still deciding on what she's going to do next year," my own mother jumped in, smiling at me, as if proud that this was the state of things. "Cora just has so many options. It's so hard for young people these days to make a decision when there are so many possibilities out there."

That was hardly the case, but I wasn't about to point out to these people that I wasn't good enough for my first-choice school, let alone any of the others.

"Well what are the options?" Mr. Carlton spoke up. He was a big, serious man with a face fixed in what was probably a permanent scowl.

"Well there are some charming private schools in the Midwest, but none near home, and I'd really like her close to home. And of course all her friends will be going to state schools, but I'd really like a private one." It was remarkable how Mom could turn a tragic situation into a less disagreeable one all for the sake of appearances. She deftly changed the subject here. "It's a pity, really, what some parents are willing to let their children do after high school. Can you believe there's a girl from Cora's class that is decided upon going to beauty school? And her mother knows. Sat right there at the graduation and told Frank all about it, as if she was proud of the girl."

Mrs. Carlton clicked her tongue disapprovingly.

"Well, for my part, I'll be happy as long as Cora doesn't end up in a cardboard box," Dad said. "She can live in the West Indies, for all I care, as long as it's got an address. Real estate will be key in the coming years."

I knew this was somehow referencing the talks he and Mr. Carlton had just had about their respective corporations, but I pounced on it as if I knew what he was talking about.

"Well, that's great, Dad, because, you know, I'd like to live abroad. And travel. You know, take a year off." My voice felt unnaturally high in the silence it occasioned.

Every eye turned on me. Even the little girl was judging me.

"One cardboard box, please!" I added with a nervous squeak.

My dad laughed heartily in the silence that had descended on the table. I gambled a look at my mother, and the look in her eyes was positively murderous. Mrs. Carlton's eyebrows were raised beyond what I thought was humanly possible. Abercrombie just looked bemused.

"Cora, the world traveler. Won't even eat green beans unless Joan douses them with sugar." Dad laughed. "I can just see her in the mountains, hunched over, eating French fries with the natives."

"Well, my boy here is going to Southern," Mr. Carlton said, clapping the kid on the back of his broad shoulders. "He's going to play water polo. For my part, I'll be happy as long as he studies law."

The parents around the table all twittered, the mothers with hands thrown daintily across their mouths, as though this was some politically incorrect joke. But it couldn't have been plainer that the man was completely and utterly serious.

And Abercrombie's face belied no resistance to this fate.

"Cora." His blue eyes were addressing me. They would have been gorgeous had it not been for his gross, self-assured smirk. "I was hoping you'd come out with me and my friends some time. Everyone is really eager to get to know you."

This could hardly be true, judging by my previous interaction with what I assumed were his "friends." But I felt my cheeks burn by the will of those cursed raging hormones and also with the knowledge that my mother was watching this scene with glee.

Damn you, cheeks!

"What a gentleman!" Mom cooed in my confused silence. "Cora, write your number down. We can't wait to get to know all you kids. Call anytime, Owen, she's simply glued to her phone." My phone was currently lost somewhere in the abyss of my pink room.

And then, scribbling my number on a napkin, Mom winked at the guy. She actually *winked* at him.

I heard my phone jingle from the floor. Even hundreds of miles away she had some kind of pull over me. I stirred clothes around, looking for the elusive phone before fishing it out from under the bed to see Rosie's exultant text.

ROSIE: Call me a wildcat, baby! Cuz it's official!!!!

She'd been taken off the wait list. That was her first-choice school.

I threw the phone at the floor where it bounced and hit the bed frame with an ominous crack, just as my unassuming mother walked in without knocking.

"What's this in your pocket, Cora?"

Weren't you supposed to be happy for your friends? So why was my blood boiling?

"Cora?" Mom had my cream-colored dress slung over one arm.

I looked at her confusedly. It couldn't be—

"You know how to do laundry?" I asked, incredulous. Joan must have given her lessons, unbeknownst to me, in preparation for this special summer away.

She ignored me. "What is all this?" she asked again, dumping a handful of seashells and the small silver flute on my desk.

I shrugged, not bothering to look up from my book. It would only please her, and I was in no mood to please my mother.

She looked at me seriously for a moment. "Are you okay? We never talked about—I mean—the other night—"

"I'm fine."

"I just mean, I didn't know if it would bring back some bad memories of—or make you think—"

"I wasn't even alive, how could I have memories of it?"

"Cora, I just—"

"Spare me the psychoanalysis, I'm fine."

She looked crestfallen. But she was in a good enough mood—left over from the successful dinner with the Carltons—that it only took her a moment to recover.

"This stuff is really dirty, Cora." She turned back to emptying the pockets of my laundry. "Really, you should wash stuff off before you go dirtying your clothes." She wiped her hands on the lace dress and her face turned wistful. "I remember when you were little, you'd always be putting leaves and things in your pockets."

I had distinct memories of Joan finding these things. She'd take my play clothes and turn the pockets inside out, scolding me repeatedly, afraid my mother would complain at the state of my clothes.

"You were always so curious, putting the strangest things in your pockets. Helicopter leaves and acorns and dandelions and those honeysuckle flowers."

"Did Joan tell you that?" I said icily.

It wasn't nice. Downright mean, really, to follow her attempt at discussing Gretel with that sarcastic remark. But we didn't talk about Gretel. That was the rule. Her own rule. And she had broken it. It was her own fault.

She was quiet for a moment before picking some invisible lint off her skirt, brushing her manicured hands over the wrinkles, and walking briskly out of the room. These days her mere presence left me annoyed and ready to quarrel with an empty room.

Good riddance, I thought. *Don't shrink my clothes.*

When she was gone, I got up and retrieved the flute from where she'd left it on the desk. I inspected it as if I was some connoisseur who could read its features. I banged it on the desk to empty the holes of sand and spit on my shirt, rubbing the mouthpiece clean before taking a tentative breath and blowing. It let out a shrill shriek that set Princess to howling downstairs.

"What the hell is that?" was my father's muffled comment from below.

I hopped down the stairs. "Do you know what this is?" I called.

Dad stopped in the second floor hall. I tossed him the pipe.

"What the hell are you doing making that kind of racket at this time of night?" he was mumbling, as he turned the thing over in his hands. "Looks like a recorder to me. Where did you get it?"

"Found it," I said.

"Just a piece of junk."

I trudged back upstairs, already regretting even asking him. I felt as though some of the magic of this little treasure had been rubbed away by revealing it to someone so mundane as my father.

Ceachtanna Snámha
SWIMMING LESSONS

USUALLY GOING TO BED MUCH EARLIER THAN MY parents and generally consuming far fewer margaritas, I was up before them in the mornings. I would grab the plastic blue pail and matching shovel from the table on the back porch. I had scoffed at my mother in the middle of the bright store in St. Louis when she had bought the preschool-blue pair in the hopes of early morning family shell hunts. But she had apparently underestimated the nighttime festivities in the old houses, so I usually found myself shoving off down the boardwalk, having emptied the previous day's finds on the table, with only Princess at my heels.

I would pick my way slowly to the pier, where Princess would sit down resignedly beside me and watch the waves with alert ears, as if squirrels and cats could be found lurking there.

The swimmer, skin wet and shiny, was always there, a few yards away, completely unaware of being watched.

Some days he was slow and gentle with the waves. But others he seemed to move with a renewed vigor, his rigid arms cutting through the waves like the biggest of Joan's Cutco knives. And I couldn't help but wonder what he was thinking. Sometimes he ducked under water completely and I looked anxiously around until he would resurface a yard farther on.

I stayed only until he turned in the distance—maybe it was two miles—and came back toward the pier. Then I'd walk back north and start my day.

One such day was marked with a big red circle on the calendar Mom kept on the purple fridge. She had given me careful instructions on what to wear and where to go before nearly pushing me out the back door. She hadn't offered to come, but I would have denied her that, anyway.

The city pool was a few blocks off Main Street, and as the day was sweltering, the pool was very crowded. I hesitated outside the tall, black, iron fence, seeing what exactly I had to contend with.

It was a giant L-shaped pool with a diving board on one end and several kiddie pools around it. There was a big, twisting water slide on one side, and mothers in lounge chairs lined the fence. Kids ran everywhere and … there they were.

A teenage girl, probably a year younger than me, was standing near a group of chattering kids. She bit her nails and looked bored, glancing at the clock every now and again. Parents showed up in a steady stream, taking towels and shoes from their kids before retreating to the outer ring of spectators. I was the oldest "kid" by about ten years.

It would have been easy to say I was too embarrassed to go. But that wasn't it. The truth was that I was downright scared. My stomach had taken up a permanent position near my shoes and the thought of getting into the pool made my skin cold.

I would have been a nervous mess, I told myself, as I stared between the rectangles in the fence.

Would have been. Well, that settled it. I had already decided I wasn't going.

I watched as the teenage girl blew her whistle and tried to get the kids to stop talking before shepherding them toward the shallow end of the pool. It was a scene too familiar for comfort.

The pool in St. Louis where Joan had taken me was eerily similar. Or maybe my memory was playing tricks on me. I had been fairly young, but I knew it was a big, crowded city pool with a flippant, disinterested teenager showing us how to hold our noses underwater. There was a boy named Rufus with red hair who I had a crush on.

It's the strangest things that a kid's memory holds onto.

That day so long ago, the first day of what was supposed to be a six-week course, I had been spectacular, or so Joan told me on the way home. We hadn't done any actual swimming, just holding our breath under water and pool safety. Pool safety. As if that was a point that I, at eight years old, needed to have hammered home one more time.

It wasn't that pool safety had ever been discussed in our house. Rather, it had *not* been discussed. *Passionately* not discussed for eighteen years. Because that was the way my mother dealt with tragedy. Or anything in life, really. If you didn't talk about it, it certainly had not happened.

So that day Joan took me to swimming lessons had been the first of its kind in my entire life. But when we arrived back at the house that afternoon, my hair stringy and wet, my mother's car was in the driveway. I didn't need to see Joan's flustered face to know that this was not going according to plan.

And when we went inside, I remember my mother unleashing a fury like I had never seen her possess before. Fury like I didn't think she had in her. She took in my wet, tousled hair and the big fluffy towel wrapped around my swimming suit. She descended on Joan like a vengeful lioness.

I was sent to my room then, but I was old enough to know that Joan had broken the rules. Caroline Manchester's child did not swim.

Not until this stupid summer at the Pink Palace.

The Pink Palace, some kind of shining beacon to my mother. She had been oddly emotional throughout my entire senior year of high school. And her solution to this premature separation anxiety was apparently to haul us out here to break the morbid fear of water that had been festering in our family since before I was born. The thing was, she wasn't all that good at facing up to things. And that's how I found myself standing *alone* at a public pool, abruptly facing a fear I'd never had to face before—a fear that I'd been encouraged *not* to face for as long as I could remember.

The swimming lesson at the Oyster Beach Public Pool was already getting into the water. *Much too fast,* I thought. But I didn't stick around to see how they fared.

When my mother asked, I told her it went great.

Bua an Dúlra
VICTORY OF NATURE

I T WAS UNCONSCIOUS NOW. THE WAY I WALKED TO my pier in the early mornings. Once there, I would see boats pulling near ports in the distance, fishermen back from early morning rounds.

The swimmer would be there, his arms spinning like windmills, churning the calm water. The waves, still weak from the night's calm would keep him bobbing ever so softly as he swam, almost like a duck, completely at home atop the waves. Some days the waves were stronger, from windy, stormy nights, and they would lap over the swimmer completely as his arms violently turned, his dark head always coming above the water eventually, shaking like a dog.

But one day I must have been a little late, because as I was approaching, the swimmer was pulling himself onto the wooden slats that sloped into the water at the end of the pier.

I stopped and walked awkwardly away. From a safe distance, I studied him, the first time I'd seen him out of the water. He was tan, with dark hair. He was solid, though not very tall, and seemed almost surreal to me. Maybe because of the way he swam, or maybe because he was soaking wet and the water made his skin gleam.

He was nothing short of gorgeous. *Hotter than a Brad Pitt knockoff*, indeed.

He breathed deeply, as though thoroughly exhausted, and sat on the edge of the pier with his legs still in the water.

When he went to stand up, I scurried away, only just realizing how awkward an interaction would be.

My dad flew home often to go to the office, so that left just my mother to deceive on the afternoons that I was "attending swimming lessons." That's when I found myself meandering back toward the old woman's house. This time, on purpose.

She would usually be outside, slumped in her rocking chair, and would call out for me to join her. Sometimes she would call to Princess, and I'd follow awkwardly, waiting for her to address me. Which she would usually do with some far-fetched tale or question about my life.

One day she ignored me completely, having summoned Princess to her side and inquiring into the dog's day. I sat down silently in my designated rocking chair and waited.

"They say a black dog is an omen of death," the old woman said, whether to myself or Princess, I couldn't be sure. "And dogs howling at the moon."

"Good thing Princess has some white and brown, too," I said, only thinly veiling my sarcasm.

"The dog days of summer are coming quite quickly," the old woman went on, as if I hadn't spoken. "It will be July before we know it, and then everything will be hot and terrible."

"What are the dog days?" I asked.

"The dog days of summer," she repeated. "It's the hottest time of the year, when the dog-star is prominent. Did you know that the sea gets crazy? Everyone is miserable. They say dogs go mad. Do you? Do you all go mad?"

Princess was unaware of being addressed. She chased a fly with loud chomps of her mouth.

"I think it's already too hot," I said. "I don't know how you stand it—being out here all day."

The old woman tore her eyes from the sea and looked at me as if I'd just tried to explain astrophysics to her. She finally spoke. "Would you find my jacket, dear?"

"You—your jacket?" I stammered.

"Yes, my coat."

She nodded seriously, so I got up, confused. I went obediently to the door and inside the dark house, wondering for the millionth time if maybe this woman wasn't completely *there*, mentally speaking.

It had become something of a routine, her asking me to find her coat or her jacket or her sweater, my pretending to search for it, and then emerging back outside empty-handed. But just after expounding on the heat? The woman wasn't all right. I went to a bookshelf to make shuffling noises, as I'd grown accustomed to doing. I ran my finger down the spines of a couple ancient-looking books (*Confessions of a Sea Maiden* and *Fairies*), waited a few moments for effect, and went back outside.

"I don't see it," I said.

"Yes, thank you for looking," the old woman replied, just like every time before.

"Are you cold?" I asked.

As always, the old woman shook her head and implored me to sit back down.

"You have quite a collection of books," I said, resuming my seat. "Have you read all those books?"

"Oh, I can't read," she said matter-of-factly.

"You—but your house is full of books!" I exclaimed. Floor-to-ceiling shelves of books!

"Yes …" the old woman mumbled.

"Were they your husband's?" I prodded, wondering why a non-reader would have quite *so many* tomes.

"What?" she appeared confused. "The-the … yes. I don't read."

I was now equally as uncomfortable as the little old woman appeared to be.

"Do you know about the Merrow, dearie?" she said, as if to change the subject.

"I don't think so," I said.

She nodded and seemed to deliberate whether to go on. I knew she would. She always did. "The Irish told each other stories about a sea creature much like the mermaid. Only she's called the Merrow." She readjusted the scarf on her head as she nodded knowingly. "They're sweet, sweet creatures. Capable of real love. Well, human love—if that can be said to be *real* love."

"Do you believe in them?" I asked skeptically.

The old woman's eyes remained fixed on a spot on the horizon. I followed her gaze. There was nothing but boats and seagulls, the normal fare of the ocean. She finally seemed to find herself and her eyes continued to rove.

"They say that love cannot overcome nature," she finally said. "Supposedly the nature of the Merrow always overcomes whatever love they held for their human man. She will always go back to her people under the sea."

Sounded to me like a cruel comment on female nature made by a bitter man.

"And the merman, oh, there are stories of mermen. Terrible stories. The mermen have cages at the bottom of the ocean in which they keep the souls of our drowned sailors and fishermen."

A chill ran through me despite my unwillingness to become involved in the story. The pale, bloated body at the pier drifted to the forefront of my mind. Souls, chained to the bottom of the ocean, fighting uselessly, perpetually against their chains, appeared in my imagination. The soul had long been gone from that bloated body when I found it.

I only then became aware of the old woman looking at me. Her eyes were narrowed and she looked at me with an intensity that I had previously only seen her use on the ocean. I felt my cheeks redden.

"They play music, too," she said. "Do you ever hear music under the water?"

I've never been under the water. I shook my head.

The old woman sighed. "I suppose one must listen for it, then. I haven't listened in a very long time. A very, very … *very* long time."

As I walked home that day, I remembered the metal recorder tucked away in my bag. That morning, I had stashed the strange instrument among my things on the off-chance that the old woman could identify it. But her stories had engrossed more than I would have liked, and I had completely forgotten to bring it up.

As it happened Owen Carlton decided to fulfill my mom's wildest dreams and invited me out with his friends one windy night. I had been sitting on my balcony, watching waves crash over my pier in the distance and recounting the Merrow story in my head (though I would never admit *that* to anyone). It was annoyingly windy, but it was the only vantage point at the Pink Palace from which I could see my pier. And then Owen had shown up at the back door. I could hear the voices below me but couldn't ascertain who it was my mom was so thrilled to see.

When she shrieked for me to "gussy up and come downstairs," I had a fairly good guess.

She nearly pushed me out the door when he invited me to join him and his friends for a bonfire on the beach.

Outside on the boardwalk, my mom probably watching from the window (but me too embarrassed to check), the twilight air was filled with awkwardness. I stumbled along next to him as he loped down the walkway. It was annoyingly close to a swagger.

I noticed with disdain that the collar to his polo shirt was popped again. It couldn't be an accident. But it was hard not to notice the way his muscled arms nearly popped out of the sleeves, as well.

I felt like I was obliged to say something, but he seemed perfectly at ease, his hands in his pockets, occasionally throwing me a smile.

"Am I dressed okay?" I finally asked, just to break the silence. In my jeans and t-shirt, I could only imagine his tiny girl friends in bikinis and whatever apparel was the standard for beach bonfires.

He grinned at me. "Yeah, you look great."

Despite my determination to despise this boy, I blushed profusely. *Damn cheeks!*

As expected, the first girl I saw—who just so happened to be Blondie—was in a tiny jean skirt and a highlighter yellow bikini top. There were sunglasses on her head despite the fact that it was nearly dark. And she was bounding up to me like an eager Labrador puppy.

Well, that part was certainly unexpected.

"Oh my god, Cora, how are you? What's up?"

"Hi," I said stupidly.

"You remember Josie?" Owen said. "And Louisa?" The bimbo was right behind her.

I nodded and hoped to God he wouldn't leave me alone with them.

He didn't. Instead, he took my hand. *My hand!* He grabbed it like this was normal and led me deeper into the group, introducing me to more people, all the while clutching my hand in his. I didn't hear a single name he said, because the throbbing sound of his hand clutching mine was drowning the entire world out. Or maybe that was my heart.

It was just the way I'd imagined Josh Watson would hold my hand. Only he never had. But I didn't want this Owen to hold my hand. *Did I?*

"I'm so glad you came out tonight," Blondie was saying as she trailed behind us. "We're really excited to have somebody new here."

"Yeah, Cora, we're going to go shopping tomorrow, do you wanna come?" the bimbo asked.

"Oh my god, yes!" Blondie exclaimed as if this was the most genius idea of the century.

"Cora, this is my buddy Sean," Owen pulled gently on my hand to steer my attention away from the girls.

A boy behind the alleged Sean came forward, veering so sharply, I assumed he was drunk. "Well if it isn't Cora Manchester!" In the light of the fire I recognized him as the formerly reticent Huston boy.

"You remember Benjamin?" Owen said.

"Miss Manchester, we met the other day." He was slurring heavily, but leering in a way that produced in me a faint urge to punch him in the stomach.

"Yeah, I remember," I said.

The Huston kid laughed. For some reason I despised his lime green popped collar more than Owen's. "And why exactly, Miss Manchester, did you fail to mention previously that Fullington Factory is owned and operated by none other than a Mr. Frank Manchester?"

I rolled my eyes. Well that explained the bimbo and Blondie simpering at my feet.

"Fullington Factory? The rainbow shoelace place?" the boy named Sean said incredulously. "Your dad owns it?"

"Isn't that, like, awesome?" the bimbo said.

Sean and the Huston boy guffawed.

"Why is it *Fullington* Factory? Who are the Fullingtons? Is it from your mother's side of the family?" I may have imagined it, but in all the hubbub, Owen looked genuinely interested in a conversation. An actual conversation. But then something occurred to the bimbo.

"Oh-migod! Do you get, like, a new pair of shoes every day?"

"Yes," I said (lied). "Yes, I do."

Owen was smirking at me, challenging my lie. But he said nothing, instead finding amusement in the bimbo's adoration. Perhaps I had underestimated Owen Carlton after all.

I later found myself sitting in a quiet nook of the gathering, next to Owen. I decided to give him the benefit of the doubt and said, "What about your father? Old or new?"

Owen laughed. "What?"

"Money," I clarified.

He laughed again. "Old. The only good kind, right?"

I laughed with him.

"What about yours?" he asked.

"It's my mom's father's business," I explained.

"Ah, smart guy, your dad, marry into it," Owen said with a teasing smile.

"Yeah, he'd be happier if I had any interest in it whatsoever. I don't. Lucky for him, my mother never did, either. Otherwise he never would have gotten to run the show. The way she was, though, my grandpa was only very happy to pass it down to a son-in-law. He didn't have any sons of his own."

"It looks like it's going that way again," Owen said. He didn't sound sarcastic, as I would have, or domineering as most boys would when speaking of such things. My grandfather's business, and his daughter's and granddaughter's complete lack of involvement or interest in it, made for some very happy relatives of mine.

"Yeah," I said. "I have a cousin who's being groomed for the business—just in case I never succeed in the husband hunt."

Owen laughed and nodded. It wasn't a gesture disgusted with this system, like I was, or outraged by it—simply accepting. This was how things went. Fathers made businesses to hand down to sons, and daughters were made to marry other sons from other families with businesses. He seemed oddly, and even refreshingly, placid. For a reason I couldn't place, it was comforting to find someone like that. So unlike myself, he wasn't pure angst and outrage, and so unlike other boys, he wasn't pure arrogant pride. I wondered what business Owen would inherit.

"Well, I know a kid born into the Heel Warehouse franchise. We could set up a merger and the two of you would have a monopoly on the American shoe market."

I laughed, a real laugh. One that started in my belly.

"A real shoe dynasty. I can set it up if you like." He was grinning and for one glorious moment, I forgot to dislike him.

I was delightfully surprised to find that, at the end of the night, Owen insisted on walking me home. Well, at the time of night when I got tired of the drunken roaring of the Huston kid and others like him and announced that I was hitting the sack.

There had been a few groans—I was magically, suddenly, not-so-mysteriously popular. Of course this had nothing at all to do with the Fullington Factory rainbow shoelace craze of the 1990's. It had made the company a pop culture icon.

I might have otherwise been bitter, but Owen had eagerly jumped up to walk me home and I felt oddly chatty.

"There's not much to do around here, is there?" I said as we made our way down the boardwalk.

He laughed. "No, not really. You can tan, swim, go shopping, tan, go shopping, and tan."

I laughed. "I haven't been doing a lot of that. But I have been walking a lot. The boardwalk gets more interesting over there." I waved in the vague direction of my pier.

Owen looked at me quizzically. "That would give my mom a heart attack to hear."

I laughed. "It's kind of interesting. There's a really old-looking pier down there. It's kind of deserted; I wonder what it was ever used for."

Owen shrugged.

"Have you ever met an old lady that lives over by the resort?" I tried again. It hit me as a stinging realization that I *still* didn't know her name. "I-I don't—I don't know her name, but she lives in this dumpy little house near the resort."

I made a mental note to ask the old woman her name the very next time I saw her.

Owen shook his head. "We don't really go over that way much. It becomes … well, it gets into a different world over there. Touristland and local territory—and that's nowhere you want to be."

I was silent because I kind of liked it.

"Especially after your little adventure," he said. "My mom would skin me alive if she heard I'd set foot down there."

He left me at the end of the walkway in our yard and waved as I paused in the middle of the stairs.

"Hey, Owen?" I called before going inside.

"Yeah?" he called back. He had his hands shoved in his pockets.

Cute or cocky? I couldn't decide.

"Do you know how to play the recorder?"

"The what?"

"Like the instrument," I said, already wishing I hadn't gone there.

He laughed. "Is that how you screen all your dates?"

Dates?

My mind was too muddled to do anything other than mutter, "Good night."

After watching him walk away in the direction of the old houses, I went inside feeling oddly cheerful, though uncertain when, in the four hours since I had left, everything had changed. I'd started the night loathing the boy in the preppy clothes. And now, apparently, it was a date, and I didn't find myself annoyed by the thought.

To my utter dismay, my mom was sitting at the dining room table when I walked in.

"What are you doing?" I demanded. "It's like two a.m."

"I wasn't about to go to bed before you got back," she replied, as if this was her common practice at home (it wasn't). "Besides, I was worried, it looks like rain."

I smiled. I was in too good a mood to fight with her. "It's just Teran trying to break free from the bottom of the ocean," I said, hopping lightly up the stairs.

"What?" she called after me.

"He's going to battle the Sea Mother!" I shouted.

An Fear Óg
THE BOY

RECUPERATING FROM MY PREVIOUS NIGHT OUT, I slept late the next morning. It was nearly noon when I finally climbed out of bed. The night at the beach had left me sticky and scratchy. I took a shower before setting out for the old lady's house, deeming it too late to go to my pier. The gorgeous swimmer would have already taken it over.

The old woman was sitting with a quilt over her legs today, a weak wind lapping at the fringe.

"How are you, Cora?" she said, her eyes on the sea.

"A little bit tired," I admitted, climbing the steps and settling into the deserted rocking chair. Princess settled at the old woman's side where a withered old hand slipped slowly out from under the quilt to pet her.

"How have your parents taken to your declaration of travel?" she asked.

I was a little embarrassed. "I haven't really asked," I admitted. "Not seriously, anyway."

"I thought you weren't going to *ask*."

"Well, I haven't *told* them yet, either," I said. My mind was occupied with running over conversations and impressions of the people I'd met the previous night, but they didn't seem like things I could mention to the old woman.

Blondie and the bimbo? They belonged to a different world than this innocent old woman.

"Did you hear about the sailors that drowned?" she asked abruptly.

I froze. I'd done more than *hear* about them.

"The boat went down weeks ago, but they're still finding the bodies." The old woman paused and glanced at me. "In fact, one of them was found by a young girl from the big houses."

I looked at her quickly. "That was me," I said, narrowing my eyes at her. "You *knew*, didn't you?"

She smiled and *nodded* as she said, "I did *not*." It was confusing to watch. "But I had my suspicions," she added.

For some inexplicable reason I was embarrassed. I felt guilty for having found that body. For having seen that man at the most vulnerable a human body could be. Utterly defenseless.

"There aren't many girls from the big houses that make a habit of walking around down here. Besides, I assumed it would be too traumatic a thing for a young girl to recall—whatever young girl was unfortunate enough to find him," she said. "So if it was yourself, I didn't wish to bring bad thoughts upon you."

Guilt flooded me. She was right. I should have been more upset. Why wasn't I more upset?

But the man had never been alive to me. He had only ever been a dead person. And maybe that's why I couldn't understand my mother's need to have this summer on the beach, her belated need for me to learn to swim. Gretel had never been alive to me. She had always been just a long-dead person.

"It was a horrible thing, wasn't it?" the old woman said, snapping me back to reality.

"What exactly happened?" I asked timidly. "I never really heard anything about it. After it happened, nobody talked about it again, like it was no big deal at all."

The woman looked at me, a long, disappointed look. A long moment for her eyes to be away from the ocean. "Nobody talked about it? You must be trying to fool me. It's all anyone's talked about."

I looked at the floor. *Nobody in the old houses,* I thought. It was a world quite different from hers, as Owen had stated all too clearly just last night.

"Even an old hermit like myself has heard of nothing but the wreck these last weeks. The boat just crashed, ran straight into an outcropping of rock, right off the side of Sele Island a few miles out."

"How terrible," I said.

But it must have come out flippantly because the old woman looked at me sharply. "It is *very* terrible. Horrific. The whole of the crew drowned."

I shook my head solemnly, trying to prove my sympathy.

"It was a fishing boat, you know. Professional fishermen, the whole of them. Peculiar way to go for locals who know the area so well. Spend most of their time out there on trawlers. Nobody understands how they could have made such a basic error of direction."

I waited for her to go on.

"Things are not generally how they seem." She smiled a grim twist of her lips as she nodded and rocked her chair gently with her feet. "Do you know what sirens are?"

And now I saw the real reason she'd brought any of this up in the first place. Visions were already hurtling through my head. The image of a rusty old bird cage stuck in the sand at the bottom of the ocean lodged in my mind. The round, floating body on the surface of the water seemed fragile and transient—the soul, the part that was forever—was a little black rock in a cage at the bottom of the ocean, plucked from the body by imaginary creatures.

"Oh, sirens are terrible, wonderful creatures." The old woman's face was tense. "Beautiful, but evil to the core." Her rocking chair made a creaking sound in the seriousness of her silence. "You know what they do, don't you? Sirens lure fishermen to their deaths."

"How?" I asked in spite of myself, gently pulling my feet up on the rail of the rocking chair to let it lull itself into a rhythmic rocking.

"They say the sirens are gorgeous half-human creatures that sing beautiful songs. Unlike anything human. Unlike anything you could imagine. So beautiful in every way that men are lured there uncontrollably. But these sirens, they're evil. They know their power; they know *exactly* what power they hold. And they lure the men in their boats, they lure them close to cliffs and rocks that sink the boats.

"They have such power over the men, these seasoned fishermen, they steer their boats right into the rocks and the cliffs. That way it looks like an accident to the rest of the world. A simple error in calculation. They say many a fisherman has lost his life to the machinations of the sirens." She left this to float on the heavy, hot wind that blew around the little house and its porch.

"I wonder what the sirens' singing would sound like," I said, remembering the recorder I'd brought. I moved to rummage in my bag and bring the curious instrument to her attention.

"Oh, I have imagined it," the old woman said, happy that I was taking interest.

"Well, would you happen to know what this—"

"Mrs. O'Leary! I'm done for the day!"

The unexpected interruption sent my thoughts reeling. My hand clutched the cold metal in my bag, as every fiber of my being clenched in embarrassment, and I slammed my feet to the ground to stop the rocking of the chair. I was embarrassed to have been caught so far outside the realms of reality as the speaker emerged from the side of the house. My mouth dropped at the sight of the young man, no older than myself, walking across the tiny, sandy lawn, wiping his hands on a handkerchief.

"Oh, I'm sorry," he said, suddenly noticing me. He slowed to an awkward amble. "I didn't know you had company."

Even at the distances from which I normally saw him, there was no mistaking this boy.

This *Brad Pitt knockoff.*

"Ronan, do come sit," the supposed Mrs. O'Leary said cheerfully. "I've made a new friend who you must meet."

The boy eyed me a little bashfully as he made his way slowly up the front stairs. He wore jeans and a t-shirt with dirt smeared on the front, and he continued to knead the pad of his thumb on the handkerchief. His dark hair was dry and tousled slightly and his unfamiliar eyes shone a dark brown at such a close distance. Dry and upright, with only the barest hint of sweat on his arms, he looked more like a normal boy and less the corporeal being at one with the ocean in the early morning.

But there was no mistaking him. This was my swimmer.

My cheeks felt like fire.

"Cora, this is Ronan," Mrs. O'Leary said. "He's just finished organizing some things in the garage and now he's on to tackle that old boat Seamus left here."

The boy stood squinting at the pair of us on the porch, the sun quite bright on the pale yellow of the house. Hoping he wouldn't recognize me, I looked bashfully at the floor, but not before noticing how perfectly adorable he was. Maybe that stemmed from the feeling that we shared some great secret, but I hoped against hope that it was a secret he was *not* aware of.

"And Ronan, this is Cora, new to our corner of the ocean, and quite the delightful new friend." The boy nodded at me slightly, uncomfortably. He was obviously just as surprised as I was to find someone else talking to his friend. "Sit down, lad, I want you two to know each other. And you must be exhausted. It's hot in that garage."

He did as he was told and sat on the top step, one leg bent with his elbow perched on top. "I was just telling Cora about the *accident*."

The boy seemed to be garnering courage from my awkward silence. "Am I to understand you don't believe it to have been an accident, Mrs. O'Leary?" He looked at the old woman with an amused expression, and slapped the dirty handkerchief over his shoulder.

"Surely not, dear." Her eyes were back on the ocean, roving the horizon, but Ronan was unfazed, speaking to her face as though she was conversing perfectly normally. He was obviously more comfortable with her odd behavior than I was. "You know as well as I what the sirens are like."

"Ah, the sirens," he said, nodding.

Though I had been harboring some daydream of being this old woman's only friend, the only listener to her outlandish tales, the huge brown eyes were a pleasant surprise. And he seemed perfectly acquainted with the stories already.

"Can you believe Cora here hasn't heard much about the accident?" Mrs. O'Leary said. "Don't know how she could have been spared. I've heard of nothing but."

Ronan looked at me again. "You're here for the summer, then," he said matter-of-factly. "In the big houses."

For some reason, it struck a nerve. I didn't want to stand out from these people, though I obviously did, and this boy was insolent enough to point it out. Emboldened by his assumption, I looked him straight back in the—beautiful, big, brown—eyes and replied, daring him to suppose anything else about my life. "Yeah, I'm here for the summer.

And yes, my parents *have* just bought a house. But I think 'big' is a relative term."

He only grinned. "You must know the girl who was down near the jetty when Rick Johnson was found," he said.

I was sick of talking about it; I was prepared to deny it.

"That was Cora herself," Mrs. O'Leary said.

Damnit.

Ronan was surprised, but not disbelieving. "How awful," he said.

"Which house is yours, Princess?" Mrs. O'Leary said, turning the conversation back to the dog as she frequently liked to do.

"The Pink Palace," I said, willing my cheeks not to blush. *Cheeks, not now!*

The pair of crinkly, old eyes flicked to the row of old houses before being pulled back to the ocean. I glanced to the north, just to verify. Yep. The Pink Palace stuck out like a sunburned elephant.

"Ah, you *do* live in the big houses, then," Mrs. O'Leary said. "Do you know the Ritz family?"

"Yes," I said, trying to avoid seeing the boy's inevitably degrading reaction.

"My Seamus was groundskeeper for them," Mrs. O'Leary said. "Many generations of Ritz have lived in that house. And my Seamus watched many of this generation grow up there."

"In the summers, at least," Ronan said quietly.

"Yes, in the winters, my Seamus loved keeping the grounds and having the place to himself. He would spend so much time there. He had a little shed at the back of the house; it was quite his little workshop. The late Mr. Ritz, you know, was a great supporter of foreign artists. He imported such lawn statues as you've never seen. My Seamus loved to tend to those—treating them for the winter weather and mending all sorts of ailments that befall them."

I kept my mouth clamped firmly shut lest I let fall just how much I knew about the famed Ritz statues.

"He was quite close to the late Mr. Ritz," the old woman went on. "The man was a very generous person, never forgot us at the holidays. They called him an industrialist. Can't say that I particularly know what that means. Such a vague way to make a fortune, wouldn't you say?"

"And, tell us, how did *your* father make his fortune?"

I stiffened and looked the brown eyes straight on. He was smirking, knowing—of all the impertinent questions—he'd lit on the one that bugged me the most.

"He runs Fullington Factory," I said with all the pride I could muster. "A Midwest shoe manufacturer that services forty-two states." At least that's what it said above the door to his office.

"Isn't that where those ridiculous shoelaces come from?" he laughed heartily.

"And what exactly do *your* parents do?" I stuffed the phrase full of as much assumption and acid as I could muster. I could tell, by the serious look on his face as he responded, that he'd understood the full of the intended insult.

"As it happens, my mom and dad run O'Brien Resort. No doubt, you couldn't help but notice it. Unfortunately, it's visible, I think, even from so far away as your *palace*."

I was red-faced and seething, and absolutely unwilling to suffer one more joke about that *damn* pink house! I sat for a moment longer, listening to Mrs. O'Leary embark on a tale of sprites. Then I interrupted her as politely as I could muster, grabbed my bag, and excused myself.

"So sorry you have to go so soon," Mrs. O'Leary called after my retreating back. "But do hurry back. Good-bye!"

The boy merely nodded as I flew down the steps, Princess at my heels.

"What a wonderful dog," I heard Mrs. O'Leary saying as I walked quickly down the boardwalk. I realized with a jolt that she had a name now. My mysterious old friend full of magical tales was a prominent figure in other people's lives, was a real person with a name in someone else's world—in this Ronan's world. I felt as if I'd just found out that some great legend was a farce. The old woman was Mrs. O'Leary. The magic was gone. The Easter Bunny wasn't real—or, rather, he *was* real, a real person in a big costume.

At home my parents were unloading deck furniture from the back of the car.

"Cora, come help, your mom's useless!"

I grumbled and went to help my dad carry the rusty items to the back porch where Mom was already pushing the pieces into different arrangements.

"Oh, honey, we just saw the Carltons and just *guess* what Mr. Carlton said!" Mom cooed. "He knows someone at St. Bernard!"

She was looking at my face expectantly, but I didn't know just what emotion to feign.

"He hasn't talked to the man in ages," Dad said, "but they used to play golf together a lot—nothing bonds old men like golf. And his man's on the board, really influential, apparently. That bodes well."

"But I didn't even apply to St. Bernard," I said.

"That's the best part!" Mom was absolutely beaming. "He thinks he could get you in without even applying!"

I unleashed a long groan, adding a severe roll of the eyes for flourish.

"Oh, yes, life is so terribly difficult," Mom said sarcastically. "Do you not care what happens to you next year? In case you hadn't noticed, there's not a single school that will have you!"

"Hush," Dad said. "Cora, St. Bernard is a great school, and the Carltons are new friends. They'd be happy to help."

"I want to take a year off," I said simply, gathering courage from the prospect of telling a proud Mrs. O'Leary how this conversation had gone.

"Don't be ridiculous," Dad said simply. I was reminded instantly of the terrible boy, Ronan, and felt all courage drain from me. *Ridiculous*, I could imagine Ronan's voice saying. He thought I was ridiculous. I deflated like an old balloon.

"Cora, you know you can't do that," Mom said. "You need to let us know what school you want to go to so that we can get you into it!"

"I don't know if you remember, since it was ages ago that you went to college," I said, "and rather pointlessly, too, considering you had your future set—"

"How dare you!" Mom cried.

"But," I plowed on, "you're supposed to *apply* to college. Which I did. And it didn't work."

"You are the most ungrateful child I've ever known!" Mom yelled. "In case you haven't noticed, your future is just as much set as anyone else in this world. As if you'll ever *not* be provided for! The least you can do for us who give you everything you want is go to college!"

"Yes, thank you for discussing this with me," I said quietly. It was a tactic I'd learned from my father in countless business calls. End the discussion politely, with force. Refuse anyone who refuses you. Then hang up. I made for the stairs quickly.

"So we'll just wait on Western. Sometimes those letters take a long time. They keep waiting to see if any spots open up." Mom seemed to be trying to convince herself. I kept silent about the rejection letter. I wasn't ready to let that out just yet. As long as we could pretend Western hadn't yet stabbed me in the heart, we could put off this fight. This life-altering decision that was bound to end in tears one way or another.

"Rosie got into LNU," I said quietly.

"See?" Mom said. "We don't have to worry yet."

Mrs. O'Leary's face came unbidden to my mind. "It doesn't matter, because I'm not going to get into Western," I said. "And if I did, I wouldn't go anyway."

I slipped inside as the yelling continued.

The next time Rosie called, I picked up simply because I was tired of ignoring her. We had been playing a game of phone tag; little did she know it was intentional on my part. I would call when I knew she was busy so that I could leave long, rambling messages. But for once, I felt up to the challenge of putting life here into words. I decided to act detached and happy, like this place was a thousand times better than any summer she could be having.

"Guess what!" was her greeting.

"What?"

"Steve and I broke up!"

"Why do you sound so happy?" I asked.

"Because I'm going out with somebody who's a hundred times better. And just *guess* what his name is!"

"I don't know," I said, making a concerted effort to sound disinterested.

"Steve!" She cackled. "He works at the mall in that store that sells, oh god, what are they called, those things that—"

"I have so much to tell you," I cut her off.

"Oh, what?"

Shit. I had nothing really. I'd just gotten sick of listening to her good news. It was making me feel unwanted, unnecessary in her life. I didn't actually have anything to say.

"Did you meet some hotties on the beach?" Rosie asked.

"Well, yeah," I said, as if this was the only thing that could be expected.

"Well, dish!" she shrieked.

"Uh … well, I met this one guy, his name's Owen. He's really hot, looks like an Abercrombie model. We're getting really close; we go out all the time, actually." I sounded more and more like my mother every day, stretching the truth farther and farther, like a goddamn Laffy Taffy. "And there's this guy who's totally adorable, he's, like, a swimmer and I see him pretty often." That much, at least, was true. I didn't mention that I saw *him* more than he saw *me*.

"*Oh*-migod! Are you gonna go out with him? The really hot guy?"

"Hey, I gotta get going, my mom's a total nutcase out here."

"Wait—I wanted to tell you about Josh."

My heart seemed to slow a few paces. "Josh Watson?" I said stupidly.

"What other Joshes do we know?" she laughed. "Just *guess* who he's going out with?"

I felt my temperature begin to rise. But it didn't stop at normal, it went right on up, setting my troublesome cheeks ablaze. "Do you talk to him much?" I asked.

"Yeah, sometimes, but Cora, guess who he's going out with—he has really short hair now. I think he must have buzzed it—"

"Rosie, I don't care," I said.

"I think he only buzzed it because Dan Lowe did his last week," she went on. "And all the girls loved it. Casey Anderson was like *throwing* herself at him. But anyway, I was at the mall to pick up Steve and I saw Josh—"

"Rosie, I do *not* care!" I yelled.

"Oh," she said quietly. "All right."

I felt guilty, but not enough to apologize. I didn't want to hear about Josh. Hearing about him reminded me that I didn't have a boyfriend. Because Josh didn't want to be my boyfriend. He'd said as much when Rosie had asked him outside the movie theater if he'd take me to dinner. Against my pleading, she'd asked him. And he'd said "No, thanks," for all the world to hear.

More importantly, hearing about Josh reminded me that I *wanted* a boyfriend. But I didn't want to be one of those girls who needed a boyfriend at all times. I couldn't say this to Rosie, because she needed a boyfriend for Christmas and New Year's and preferably a brand new one for Valentine's Day. I didn't want to be like that. But I felt like that now.

"I'm gonna go," I finally said.

"Okay, call me, okay?" She was light and flippant again. It was hard to fight with Rosie. "I have to tell you all about Steve. The new one, he's *so* much cooler than Steve Debrowski. And most people call him *Steven*. Like Steve-*en*. I think that's *so* much more mature, you know?"

"Yeah, I'll call you," I lied.

Ag Casadh le Seamus
MEETING SEAMUS

THAT SUMMER, THE SAND WAS SUFFOCATING. IT would gather in my shoes and in the folds of my clothes, only to pile up in the laundry room where I shook them out. It stuck to my hands and my hair, and even Princess's ears. Tiny rivulets gathered in the house where the wind pushed it a little farther in every time someone opened the door.

I didn't go to the pier in the morning anymore. The last thing I wanted was to run into the annoyingly cute jerk, Ronan.

It was proving too easy to hide from my parents that I wasn't going to swimming lessons. Dad flew around a lot for business and even when he was here, he was either tucked in his room on his laptop, on the phone or gone golfing. Mom was in her own world of antique shops and her new B.F.F. Linda Carlton, and I spent as much time as possible away from the Pink Palace.

I started sleeping late and meandering toward Mrs. O'Leary's house in the afternoon, generally checking the vicinity for any sign of Ronan before joining the old woman on the porch. If he was there, I'd spin around and quickly make my exit before they saw me.

One such day, however, Princess bounded ahead of me and joined Mrs. O'Leary and Ronan on the porch before I could stop her.

"Hello there, dear girl," I heard Mrs. O'Leary greeting her.

I briefly considered walking home and pretending Princess had run away from me, but she was my dad's favorite daughter and I didn't dare face him without her safely in tow.

Mrs. O'Leary was delighted to see me.

"Come sit, dear," the old woman said. "We were just discussing kelpies and changelings."

I turned a delightfully amused face at Ronan, hoping to see him embarrassed to be caught in a world of fantasy, but his face was impassive, completely unperturbed. Those were the hardest boys to ignore: the ones that weren't concerned with your opinion of them, not afraid to be caught listening to fairytales. I wasn't exactly used to boys being concerned with my opinions of them, but I was used to them haranguing me for Rosie's opinion, and, thus, attempting to please me by association.

To my utter dismay, Ronan stood and made a gesture for me to sit in the rocking chair. I mumbled a polite refusal, but Mrs. O'Leary entreated him to fetch her jacket and ordered me to sit. Ronan disappeared into the little house.

"What's on your mind, dear?" Mrs. O'Leary asked me, her eyes on the ocean.

"Not much," I said. I couldn't help wondering if Ronan was actually looking for the jacket inside or just playing along like I did. "What's on yours?"

She sighed deeply and fiddled with the silk scarf over her hair. "What always is," she said simply.

I was about to inquire after what this could be, but there was rarely a need for that with Mrs. O'Leary. She went on without aid.

"Do you know of Shoney, dearie?"

I shook my head. "What's that?"

"They say he was a spirit that dwelled in the waters near Scotland. Seonaidh, my Seamus would call him. Seamus had a great love of ale; it was the Celt in him. Do you know, people used to wade into the water and give an offering of ale to Shoney? It was meant to appease him and secure them a good harvest."

I thought of drunken old Scottish men stumbling into the ocean and draining buckets of beer—draining just as much into their stomachs as the water. I didn't say as much.

"But of course my Seamus liked to make a mockery of it. He was Irish, you know. He would go into the water with his ale and drink it all down—some might say that was a slight to Shoney."

"I don't think he'd mind," I mumbled.

"Seamus liked to enjoy his ale, right here on this beach. You know, that is how we met. Me, swimming along minding my own business, and my Seamus roughhousing with ale and good friends."

So she had met her husband when he was stark raving drunk. *How quaint.*

"I'd seen him before, of course. Every day, when I was swimming." She looked at me out of the corner of her eye, possibly to see if I was listening. The parallels of the story were unsettling. Swimmers, spying, crushes, wanting to see the world? Who exactly had this old woman been talking to? *Shit*—did Ronan know more than he was letting on? Or was this woman just clairvoyant?

"But it took me a long time to make the change. To tell my mother. So when I came to the beach and met him, there he was with his ale. He was very taken with me. We moved into this little house and had a grand life altogether. Of course, as nature will do—it stifles things. Feelings. I started to yearn for a return to the water, but my Seamus kept me here."

The statement was chilling. As was the way she said it.

"You don't swim anymore?" I asked feebly.

The old woman started and stared at me for a long moment before laughing. "No, no." The laugh faded and she spoke seriously again, though this time without looking at me. "That is not to say that had I the choice once more, I would not make the same decision."

It was an echo of things she'd told me weeks ago, during one of our first talks. "To … to 'see the world,' you mean?"

"Yes, oh yes."

"Is this it?" Ronan reappeared then with a deep purple sweater.

Mrs. O'Leary looked up rather hopefully but shook her head. "No, I am afraid not."

Ronan slung the sweater across the porch banister, and the old lady settled down into her seat with a sigh. The scene had a practiced air.

"You can have your chair back," I said, rising. I had been wandering in a salty dreamland and his reappearance had dropped me back into the stifling world of teenage angst. I was determined not to be indebted to this jerk on *any* account.

But he shook his head. "I'm going to get back to work." For the first time I noticed the pile of tools and metal objects strewn about the far end of the porch. He settled on the floor among them and immediately began prodding and twisting unfamiliar gadgets.

"Ronan is fixing my Seamus's collection," Mrs. O'Leary explained. "Fishing gear. All know I couldn't be called upon to give the name or use of a single one of those things. I told him he could have it all if he fixed it."

"Delightful," I said, to please her. Ronan looked up and gave me a tight-lipped smile.

"He's a fantastic fisherman, Ronan is," Mrs. O'Leary said.

"Are you?" I said overly sweetly.

"Almost as good as he swims. He swims quite fabulously."

"Do you?" I threw the same feigned smirk at him again.

"Every morning," he said. I was startled out of my sarcasm. It could have been a simple retort to match my sarcasm—or it could have been a hint that he knew I was a semi-stalker. I preferred the term *admirer*. But any admiration was definitely gone now.

In any event, I decided to stay quiet until Mrs. O'Leary finished heralding Ronan's various merits.

"He's going to Ireland this year," she said. Her brows furrowed and her eyes grew sad. "He's getting so very, very old. How very many years he's seen and yet still so young."

Not only did that not make sense, but Ronan couldn't have been older than me. *Drama queen*, I thought.

"It would have been a great comfort to my Seamus," Mrs. O'Leary went on, "seeing the return of so many to the homeland. So many leave, never to return." Her eyes appeared to be welling up. A sincere display of emotion at the memory of her husband, I assumed. "Seamus was a proud Irishman. As Ronan here. Aren't you, lad?"

"My parents are Irish," Ronan clarified.

"You could tell, of course, by the name," Mrs. O'Leary went on. "Such a blatantly Irish one his father chose." She wiped at one of her eyes.

I made a noncommittal noise, trying to sound less interested than I was. But Ronan offered no further commentary.

"What about you, dear?" Mrs. O'Leary said. She sniffed softly. "Cora. *Cora*." She rolled the name around. "It is a strangely formal name for a young girl, isn't it?"

"It's an old family name," I explained a little defensively. When people would question my name (which was often) I instinctively felt they were criticizing it. And I was sure that presumptuous boy in the corner was using it to validate his assumptions about my family's excessive pride. "It goes back several generations on my mom's side." I again waited in vain for him to offer some sarcastic comment.

Nothing happened, but Mrs. O'Leary used the topic to springboard into a monologue on generations of faeries. I took the opportunity to sort out my complicated feelings about this difficult boy. He sure looked nice enough sitting there fixing rusty metal things. More than nice, actually. He was the definition of hot. In a way completely different than Owen Carlton. Owen knew he was hot. But Ronan acted like it was the last thing on his mind. He merely went about his work, occasionally looking up politely at Mrs. O'Leary to show the attention he was paying her.

But I couldn't get past the feeling that he looked at me with amusement, as if I was there solely to provide him with a few laughs.

My mother's dream kept coming true. Owen kept inviting me to spend time with him and his friends, and out of a lack of anything better to do, I always accepted. I didn't want to admit it to anyone, least of all myself, but I wasn't so very against Owen's presence anymore. Filthy rich and dressed to the nines or not, he was polite and sometimes even funny. I just wished it didn't please my mother so much.

He was always a gentleman, walking me home when it was late, and though he talked a bit too often of water polo, it was better conversation than anything Blondie or the bimbo could offer. All in all, he helped the weeks flutter away instead of dragging on like I'd expected them to.

Having stopped going to the pier altogether in the mornings, I felt a pang of regret for losing my special spot. So it became custom for me to wander there at dusk. I'd stay until a little after dark, and wander back home when I was sure my mother would be asleep—passing out from the margaritas—and my father, if in town, would be in the process of passing out in front of the TV.

One such night Princess came with me. I was sitting as far out on the pier as possible without sinking with the flimsy end and threw a tennis ball repeatedly onto the beach. Princess would run down the pier and find the ball in the sand before running back and dropping it at my feet. Then I'd throw it again and wait for her to come bounding back.

Twenty minutes into the game, she found something in the sand that wasn't her tennis ball. She dug at it for a minute before dislodging it and running to drop it at my feet. It was another recorder.

I picked it up as Princess bounded back for the tennis ball. The recorder was wet and sandy, like the last one I'd found, and now covered in dog drool. This one was a dull bronze color. I wiped it on my t-shirt and, throwing caution to the wind, blew into it. It puffed sand and dirt out before making a loud off-pitch screech. Princess approached me hesitantly, her ears perked and dropped her ball at my feet.

I wasn't quick enough and the ball rolled straight off the wooden plank into the water. Princess and I both stared longingly at it, bobbing in the water, just over arm's length away.

"Sorry, girl," I said. "It's a goner."

Suddenly, a head popped out of the water.

My lungs let loose. I screamed like I'd never screamed before.

The head ducked back beneath the water.

What are the odds one person can come across two dead bodies in the span of weeks? I calmed my lungs. *What in the world was that?* Princess was staring, her head slightly cocked, at the space where the head had disappeared.

The shiny, brown head poked above water again, this time just the eyes. When it realized the loud noise had subsided, its nose appeared and nudged the tennis ball toward the pier. Then it ducked back beneath the water. It was a *seal!*

I had never seen a seal outside the zoo before, but its round, brown head with the pointy nose and long whiskers were unmistakable.

The seal once again poked its head hesitantly above the water—just its brown eyes visible. When it decided I was definitely done with the noise, its whole head appeared, and it nudged the ball again. It kept on until the ball was within my reach, then it looked right up at me.

It had huge brown eyes, perfectly round. The moon was small yet tiny bits of light glinted in the seal's eyes.

I was too afraid to reach for the ball with the strange animal so close. As if in understanding, the seal slowly started to swim away. It stopped several times to turn around and look back, as though to check if I'd reached for the ball yet, before disappearing in the dark.

I hesitated. I was sure it was still out there, watching us. I finally leaned over and, stretching as far as I could, snatched the ball as quickly as possible.

Ball safely in hand, I looked all around us out at the dark water. How many were out there, just out of my sight?

Seacht Deora
SEVEN TEARS

O NE NIGHT OWEN INVITED ME TO A PARTY AT the Ritz house. The Mr. and Mrs. were to be at the family's year-round home in Virginia seeing an ill relative, and the youngest Ritz boy, a flighty, skinny thing of sixteen, was trying his very best to impress the older kids.

I walked there with Owen, hand-in-hand, which was beginning to happen with more frequency, and Blondie and the bimbo met us on the way. I'd long since ceased feeling insecure when I saw them on the way to a social event. Blondie was in tight jeans and a tube top to show off her impeccable tan, and the bimbo was in a strapless dress tighter and shorter than any I'd seen before. Meanwhile I was in jeans and my one and only "nice" top—a frilly little pink number my mother had picked out when I was fifteen. But it was *my* hand Owen was holding.

My confidence that couldn't be shaken.

Ritz Manor was absolutely glowing, the front door thrown open with giggling teenagers in various states of inebriation stumbling out. I had never known there to be so many teenagers in the area. But many were familiar. Those that were usually difficult to stomach were even more so after a few shots of Grey Goose.

On the whole, I was doing fairly well dealing with the despised. Blondie disappeared in the arms of a redheaded boy and the bimbo trailed Benjamin Huston relentlessly as he obviously tried to lose her among the masses. Owen was quick to offer me anything I wanted, but I declined most, enjoying his attentions, but hoping to be able to escape the rowdy, headache-inducing mess fairly soon.

I had wandered into the sitting room where there were huge bay windows looking down to the back of the house. The backyard sloped down gently, and from this vantage point, you could see all the way down to the sea. The in-ground pool took up a good half of the yard, huge islands with giant palm trees sprinkled throughout it. But it was the little shed just barely visible behind the pool house that I was looking for. There was no other structure so tiny or shabby on the premises—this had to be where Seamus O'Leary had kept shop all those years ago.

When a boy I knew only as Sean walked by holding hands with a tan girl and declared that he was "going upstairs to get some," I made my disgusted exit. Owen followed me outside to the front yard where someone was attempting to climb to the top of the largest of the Ritz statues.

"Don't go," Owen pleaded with me, as we walked down the front walk.

"I'm really tired," I said. I smiled at him, wanting him to know it wasn't him I couldn't stand—just his friends.

"I swear it'll get better," he promised. "Once they start passing out, it quiets down."

I laughed, a smart retort on my tongue, but before I knew it, my tongue was otherwise employed. It wasn't the most romantic of scenes, and the guy on top of the bronze Napoleon made lewd, albeit slurred, comments, but I was too shocked to care.

He kissed me softly at first, waiting for my approval, and when he found it, he slid his arms around my waist and I was too turned around to know exactly what to do with my hands, which lay limply on his arms.

He finally pulled away (to my disappointment, I will admit) and looked at me beseechingly. "Come back inside." He smiled, and I smiled. Then he took my hand, and I was quite at a loss to do any thinking for myself.

The fun continued on the couch in Mr. Ritz's library—for how long, I don't know—until the bimbo interrupted.

"Cora!" she shrieked. "C'mere, I need you!"

"What is it?" I asked, wrenching my mouth away from Owen's quite against my own will. Her hair and clothes were disheveled and she looked positively terrified, not to mention she was slurring something awful.

"Josie's barfing, and I d-d-dunno whata do!"

I groaned and made to get up, but Owen held me tight. "She'll be fine," he said.

"No-no-no, Marshall Ritz said she's gotta go outside 'cause 'cause the bathroom's clean," the bimbo said.

I stood up, but Owen held onto my arm. "Stay," he said.

"I'm just going to make sure she's okay," I insisted.

"Cora—"

"She could be really sick." And as I followed the bimbo upstairs, I thought I saw a passing look of anger on Owen's face. We went to the master bathroom where Blondie was curled on the floor, quite unconscious. Luckily she woke up when we came in and I did my best to clean the bathroom—and her—to Marshall Ritz's satisfaction, all the while soothing the bimbo's worries that she would lose her dinner, too.

When Blondie and the bimbo were cleaned up, mentally and physically, they both crawled into the master bed where they were quite on the way to falling asleep as I set a small waste can from the bathroom by the bed and went downstairs. The library looked just as I had left it—double doors flung open with various couples strewn about couches and on the floor. But one thing was amiss. Owen wasn't alone and he sure as hell wasn't *talking* to the girl he had pinned between him and the baby grand piano.

I left the house as fast as I could without bringing attention to myself and willing the tears not to come. Even as I ran home down the boardwalk, I felt foolish as my eyes watered. It wasn't as though he was my boyfriend, and it wasn't as though he'd ever even declared feelings for me. But God, it hurt all the same.

He'd held my hand. He'd *kissed* me! It wasn't my *first* kiss, but it was definitely the first that hadn't included Spin the Bottle.

Princess bounded down the back steps to meet me, but I stopped short. The Pink Palace's dining room lights were on and I could hear laughter inside. Of course Oyster Beach's finest adults would be wining and dining while its finest youth poisoned themselves just down the way.

Apparently these people *never* grew up!

I turned on my heel and ran to the only place I could guarantee would be empty—my pier. Princess trotted loyally at my heels.

As expected, the pier was quite deserted. The waves were extremely choppy, a storm in the forecast, and the end of the pier wobbled a little more than usual. I plopped down, but couldn't bring myself to let the tears fall freely. What a pathetic thing to cry about. I laid on my stomach and hung my head over the edge of the splintery wood, my hands under my neck, the uncomfortable tears falling warm down my cheeks and dripping into the cold waves below as I tried desperately to stifle them.

One. Two. The tears made tiny circles before being swallowed by a wave. The warm tears and cold, salty spray mixed to make my face feel clammy. My dad always said crying was a waste of energy. *Three.* I felt like crying just to spite him! But as a consequence of being raised by such a father, crying made me feel vulnerable and childish, two things both my parents fervently discouraged. *Four.* Sniffing and sobbing I cursed everything that came to mind. The Ritzes, my parents, Rosie, Western University, St. Bernard's damned bribable board members. But my thoughts stayed carefully far from Owen Carlton. To let him cross my mind while I cried would be to admit that a boy, a boy my mind had warned me against while my hormones ran wild, had gotten the better of me. *Five.* But he *had* gotten the better of me. I had been convinced—I who had always considered myself above any dependence on boys—*I* had been easily convinced that he liked me. He had never wanted me—any girl would do. I knew that. And somehow he had wheedled his way through my defenses. The teardrops made fat, temporary circles before being devoured by the growing unrest of the ocean. *Six.* Right then, on the pier, all I could feel was alone. I didn't ever feel alone—I was independent—independent girls didn't feel alone. That's what I told myself. But somewhere along the way Owen Carlton had managed to create in me a small hole where I wanted to be wanted. *Seven.*

A sudden splash ripped me out of my reverie and the series of inhuman squeals and barks that followed sent my heart thumping. If a dog could cry for help it would sound like that—

"Princess?"

I ran to the end of the pier, frantically reaching, grabbing at the terrified face of my sweet, sweet, innocent dog. I reached and reached, as far out as I could. Just a few feet farther Princess flailed and bobbed, piercing the night with her short, moaning howls.

Before I could form a rational thought or feel anything other than pure terror, there was a loud thumping on the pier behind me and another, more deliberate splash that produced a figure next to Princess. I fell to my knees and watched breathlessly as he scooped Princess up into his arms and dispatched her on the pier next to me.

Princess got up and commenced a furious shaking of her wet fur, as I hugged and kissed her, surprised to be crying for reasons quite unrelated to Owen Carlton now.

Ronan pulled himself out of the angry water onto the edge of the pier, where he sat breathing heavily and completely soaked. The wobbly pier shook beneath us in the excitement. It was probably the most weight it had held in decades.

"What's a dog doing on the goddamn jetty?" Ronan was fully dressed, but his t-shirt was soaked and plastered to his chest now, his khakis dark and dripping. All he'd deposited before jumping in were his tennis shoes, which sat tauntingly dry beside him.

"What did you do?" I said softly to Princess. "You know you can't swim! What were you thinking?" She rubbed her head against my dry shirt. She *hated* when her ears got wet! I held her close to me and hazarded glances at Ronan, knowing that thanks were in order but not knowing quite how to go about it.

"Thank you," I finally said, quietly, slowly. It was sincere, but thanks so frequently have the tendency to sound flippant. So I said it one more time for good measure.

He was silent and didn't even acknowledge I'd spoken. After a few more moments of staring out at the ocean in a Mrs. O'Leary fashion, he finally said, "Why didn't you save her?"

When I didn't answer, he looked at me. His hair was messed up, dripping over his forehead but his brown eyes were oddly piercing. "Are you so used to everyone doing everything for you that you wouldn't even save your own dog?"

My mouth was empty, but I was crying for too many reasons now. I wanted to appear calm and proud and look him square in the eyes. Instead my shoulders crumpled, and I looked down at Princess.

He grabbed his shoes and walked away.

Ainm Rónán
RONAN'S NAME

I DIDN'T TELL MY PARENTS ABOUT THE INCIDENT at the pier. It would lead to questions that would lead to the incident at the Ritzes' which would lead to prodding about Owen.

I dried Princess with a towel when we got home, and muttered a few acceptable noncommittal answers to my mother's insufferable question about the party. (*"No*, all the other girls *weren't* wearing dresses.")

"How did the baby get all wet?" I heard my dad ask as I climbed the stairs two at a time.

Luckily, when I got up the next morning, he had already left for the airport.

I avoided Owen carefully in the days following, and I was confused to find I didn't see Ronan around Mrs. O'Leary's. I felt that thanks and further explanation were necessary, but I struggled to form the words in my head.

I still went to Mrs. O'Leary's daily, even more eagerly now that Owen was gone and she was my only source of entertainment. But Ronan was usually busy elsewhere, as she would tell me.

One day near the end of June, I outlasted Mrs. O'Leary on the porch. It was the first time I'd stayed until sunset, and she declared her intention to go inside. After she locked up, I lingered on the porch, taking advantage of the view of the sunset the little porch afforded. It faced north, giving a split view of the ocean and the endless row of mansions, the sun settling quietly behind the big houses and throwing an orange glow over their impeccable white paint.

Well, all but ours. The Pink Palace sat in a soft pinky-orange glow, taunting me.

I was so absorbed in it, I didn't hear Ronan come out of the garage. When I noticed him, he was standing in the grass, wiping his hands on a towel and watching me. Startled, I blushed.

"Has Mrs. O'Leary already gone inside?" he said.

I nodded.

"She had a rough day today," he said. "She asked me to get her jacket three times."

I nodded, debating whether it was okay to start a conversation with him given our past. I wanted to explain that embarrassing night on the pier, or as he called it, the jetty, but I couldn't. So if he stayed away from that topic, then I could be civil.

"What's that about?" I asked. "She does that to me a lot."

He looked at me with squinted eyes, as if assessing whether or not I was trustworthy. But he finally looked resigned and said, "I don't really know. She's had a rough time since Mr. O'Leary died."

I nodded sympathetically, as if I could possibly know how that felt.

"He did everything around the house," Ronan went on. "And when he died, she would say she didn't know where anything was anymore. That's why my parents set me up to help her go through the house, clear things out. She talks about this jacket that she says her husband must have left somewhere, some days she says he hid it. But I've been through that house several times over, and no matter what I find, it's never the right one." He paused. "I don't know if you've noticed, but she's never completely *here* anymore."

"I have noticed," I said. I also couldn't help noticing this boy was being suspiciously nice to me, compared to the last time we'd met.

"Well, that's recent. She isn't usually like that."

"How long has he been dead?" I asked.

"About ten years," he said. There was a pause, again, as if he was contemplating my merit. Then he finally said, "You know, my name *isn't* Ronan."

I gaped at him. After a few moments of fuzzy silence, I spluttered, "What?"

"My name isn't Ronan," he said again. "She's been calling me that for years." He looked at my confused face a moment longer, then laughed. "My name's Rory," he said with an amused grin. "It's a pleasure to meet you." He offered his hand.

I shook it, perplexed. "Why does she call you Ronan?"

He shrugged. "I don't know if she thinks I'm someone else or if she just gets confused. It's been going on so long, maybe she just doesn't remember that it's not my name."

"It doesn't scare you?" I asked. "I mean, that she thinks you're someone else …"

He shook his head. "She had a son named Ronan. Years and years ago she had a baby, a boy that they named Ronan. He disappeared when he was just a few months old. A few years later she had another baby, but it didn't live more than a day. She was really sick after that. And then a little while after her husband died, she started calling me Ronan. I think it's all just tangled up in her mind."

I was shocked. "The baby disappeared?"

He shrugged. "Nobody knows what happened to it. Some say it must have drowned when she and Seamus weren't looking."

A lump crept up my throat. *Nobody was looking.* How many times had I heard that murmured behind my back?

"All anyone knows is that he disappeared without an explanation." He could see I was unsettled. "Anyway, I'm used to it—her calling me Ronan."

I swallowed a few times. "You … you never correct her?"

He shrugged. "I did early on. My mom tried talking to her. We don't think that she actually believes I'm her son. She's just confused. I have a lot of brothers. She just gets names mixed up. And now that it's been going on so long, well, she's probably just forgotten."

Having opened up this much, I wasn't afraid to ask the question I was too scared to ask Mrs. O'Leary herself. "How did her husband die?"

Ronan—uh … Rory—sighed. "At sea. In a little dory."

"What's a dory?"

Despite the serious countenance of his face, a flash of amusement passed through his eyes. "It's a boat," he said. "A tiny little boat. Seamus liked to fish alone, but all he had was that little dory. And one day he didn't come back. The boat was never found." Rory looked at me and I realized my mouth was hanging open. "Of course, as you've seen yourself, boating accidents aren't uncommon around here. But there was a lot of discussion about whether or not it was suicide. Whether their marriage had fallen apart after the death of their children."

Mrs. O'Leary had told me nature conquers the feelings of the Merrow. Had it conquered her feelings? Had it stifled her own feelings for her husband?

"You know how people talk," Ronan—Rory—said absently.

I knew all too well how people talked. But in my experience, they whispered. Whispered behind your back, when they thought you weren't listening, not wanting to disturb the children, of course.

Then something occurred to me. "She's always looking," I said. "She never stopped searching the ocean. Like he's lost at sea. *She's* lost at sea."

He nodded and we lapsed into silence. To be left alone like poor Mrs. O'Leary, in a house you couldn't run, with nobody to visit but Rory, whose name you didn't even know, and a strange, disinterested girl who thought your stories were proof that you were psychologically unstable.

I felt like an absolute *jerk*.

"You're here late," Rory finally said.

I nodded, trying to gather my thoughts into the same hemisphere. "I was just leaving and got distracted by this view of the sunset."

He turned to see where I gestured. "I would think you would be used to it," he said. "Don't all the big houses have gigantic windows facing west for this exact purpose?"

A retort was on my tongue, but he went on. "My room has a window with a glorious view of the resort pool. There are no walls thick enough to keep out the shrieking in the kiddie pool at seven a.m."

I laughed. "Is that why you're up so early?" It was out before I could stop it. Meant as a joke, in another conversation with any other person in the world, it would have sounded mocking and light. My cheeks were on fire and other random, embarrassment-aware parts of my body burned.

Stupid cheeks. Stupid cheeks. Stupid cheeks! It was like guilt, painted right across my face in the brightest paint possible.

Rory turned around, and I held my breath, waiting for a sudden realization of my early-morning stalking or a quick fleeing from my sight, or at the very least some scathing remark about hard work.

Instead he said, "I've been wanting to tell you—I'm really sorry I was rude the other night. That night at the jetty—with your dog. I really wanted to apologize. I was in a bad mood already, and then I just—but I mean, it happened so quick, I shouldn't have assumed you weren't going to …"

I shrugged. "It's okay." I was torn between not telling this boy anything about me, not to gratify him with reasons, or on the other hand spilling all to the newfound confidante, this new boy I felt I had met only moments before, this Rory. The boy had transformed along with his name.

"I thought I had to act quick, you know, just in case you had ideas to let the poor pup drown." He said it with a smile to let me know he was teasing. He had no idea how that last word cut through me.

I forced myself to smile back and then said evenly, "I can't swim."

He was quiet for a moment, shocked by my sudden revelation, no doubt. "Is that all?" he finally said with a smile.

Of course it wasn't, but I wasn't about to go that far. "Yes, I have no death wishes for Princess," I said.

He smiled, seemed to deliberate for a second and then said, "You know, I can teach you to swim."

My cheeks flushed. *Does he know? Is that his way of telling me that he knows?*

I wanted to blurt out that I wasn't a stalker, but at the same time, visions of the two of us swimming the ocean in the morning drifted at the forefront of my consciousness and many parts of my body were burning. But I never got to answer. I was interrupted by the appearance of someone on the boardwalk.

The thin girl skipped over to Rory and embraced him, lightly kissing him on the cheek. The scene unfolded in front of me like a stack of bricks tumbling onto my head.

I waited for an introduction, but an explanation was unnecessary. The girl slipped her arm around Rory's lower back and put her head on his shoulder. It was the blonde, leggy girl with pigtails. The one who knew her way around so well—the one who didn't get lost. She was probably a local, and she probably knew how to swim, too.

"How was your day?" The girl broke the silence, throwing me a furtive look while addressing Rory. She may or may not have recognized me, but either way she was clear about her utter lack of interest in me. "I wondered what was taking so long."

"Hey, Jen, this is Cora," Rory said.

"Hi," I said.

She merely looked at me.

"Jen," Rory said gently, pausing a moment, "Cora is the one who found Rick."

The girl's face dropped. She turned to look me up and down. She finally said, "What were you doing so far south?" It felt like an accusation.

"I was just walking," I said, my traitor cheeks turning red. Once again, that guilty feeling rose in me. As if I had been doing something wrong by being at the pier when that body surfaced. "I was just walking. You know, wandering." I was blabbering nervously; this could only end badly.

"Wandering a little far from home, weren't you?"

"I just walk a lot," I heard myself say, as if from outside my own body. "Nowhere in particular, and then I just stumbled upon the pier and I saw something big and puffy in the water …"

"Which would be my brother," she interrupted icily.

My face flooded red. "Your brother?" My forehead, my nose, my lips, my ears. "Oh, my god. I'm so sorry." Any hotter and there would have been flames erupting from my face. "I just saw … it was so sad. All those men, and your brother. Mrs. O'Leary said it was the sirens' fault …"

"The *what*?"

Shit. Shit. Shit.

Rory jumped in deftly. "You know her, with her tales and things."

"Yeah, and I'm sure Rick was too busy texting Big Bird to watch where the goddamn boat was going," Jen said. "Bet he drove right into Atlantis."

Rory slipped an arm around her back and steered her toward the boardwalk. He shrugged and shot me a sympathetic smile meant to reassure me as he walked her quickly away.

I twirled around in frustration. *Stupid,* stupid *Cora! Learn to control your words!*

Motion from the cloudy window at the top of Mrs. O'Leary's little yellow house caught my eye. It was Mrs. O'Leary, up in the attic. I briefly wondered what she was doing up there by herself. She moved out of sight again. I decided using your own attic wasn't a crime and whirled back around to go home.

On the way, I walked in the sand, kicking up dusty clouds to keep myself occupied. It wasn't enough and I couldn't help but wonder what the sinking feeling in my stomach was. I didn't think it had anything to do with my terrible conversational skills. I was used to embarrassing myself. But every time I saw it in my head—Ronan's arm around the Jen girl—my stomach sank like I was on a roller coaster.

What a crappy roller coaster.

Selkies
SELKIES

I T WAS ONLY A MATTER OF TIME BEFORE I WAS forced into the presence of Owen Carlton again, and unfortunately for me, my mom was there, too. "Would you excuse us, Mrs. Manchester?" he said in that polite voice of his that he reserved for talking to adults. "I've been dying to speak with Cora alone."

Mom was beaming as she shooed us into privacy. It was the Carltons' own dinner party that I'd been wrangled into attending, and so he had the upper hand in the situation. Not knowing the terrain, I had unknowingly followed my mother into the pool hall—Owen's own den. Now he led me out of the room and up an impressive set of stairs.

"I was just getting ready to go," I faltered, caught up in the grandeur of the portraits of the Carlton family strung along the staircase.

"You just got here," he said matter-of-factly.

He took my hand and though I pulled some at the outset, he was persistent and I saw little point in resisting. We appeared in what resembled a second game room on the second floor. This one was smaller, free of a pool table, but complete with air hockey and foosball.

He led me over to the air hockey table where he spun around and pinned my waist against the table. He grinned and said, "Long time no see," before pressing his lips against mine.

I wrenched my face away. "Are you kidding me?" I said.

"Cora," he sighed. "I've been dying to see you ever since that party."

"Oh, you must have misplaced my number," I said, gathering my sarcastic strength from somewhere in the depths of my teen-angst-filled soul.

"No, I just thought you were going to be pissed at me," he said.

"You're clairvoyant," I replied.

"Cora." He wouldn't budge, my body pressed firmly between the foosball table and his annoyingly chiseled body, my face inches from his. "I miss you."

My remark about the painful length of six days was lost somewhere in my throat where a strange unwanted lump was forming. I was saved the trouble of replying by the appearance of Blondie, leading her redheaded male by the hand.

"Whoa, I didn't know this room was taken," Blondie giggled.

"Seriously, guys?" Owen said, leaning away from me, but keeping a firm grip on my hand. "Our parents are downstairs. That's sick."

Blondie giggled again and shrugged, but whatever her plans were, they were destroyed by the bimbo's appearance and her insisting upon a match of foosball.

"Cora and I will take on any of you," Owen said with that easygoing nature that had succeeded in bringing down my guard the first time around. He snaked an arm around my back, and while I went to pull away, the image of the leggy blonde with pigtails popped into my head. *Jen.* She had a name now.

Rory. It was familiar and comfortable, like I had known his name all along. The boy, Ronan, was a disagreeable thing of the past. Rory was somebody new, someone I could talk to. Rory was—Rory and Jen.

I let Owen lead me to the foosball table with a hand on the small of my back.

"Ronan is finished in the garage," Mrs. O'Leary told me one day.

I had been hoping conversation would stay clear of him, but I felt my heart shift just a miniscule amount at the thought of him not hanging around Mrs. O'Leary's anymore.

The old woman seemed nervous and fidgety today, at least more so than usual. "He's getting so old. So much older than a boy of his age should be."

I didn't even try to unravel that logic.

"He'll be starting on the house now," she went on. "There's so much my husband left sitting around. One can't find a thing in all of it."

I nodded absently, silently grateful I'd still see Rory, however distantly.

"He was a messy man, my Seamus. But I wouldn't have had him any other way."

"Are you cleaning the house up for something, Mrs. O'Leary?" I asked. I had been wondering where this project was leading, what would become of the old woman when her handyman went off to Europe as he was scheduled to do in the fall. She mentioned his leaving sometimes, but only in passing.

Whatever her motive, Mrs. O'Leary wasn't letting me in on it. "Things belong in a place," she said cryptically. "You have to let things go to their places."

I nodded as if I had any inkling of her meaning.

"Yes, I do think everything has a place," she went on. "Yourself included."

Huh? This had to be one of those life-direction lectures that had permeated my life all of the last year of high school via teachers and my parents and Rosie's parents. But for some reason, the looming lecture coming from this frail old woman didn't sound threatening or even boring. In any event, my intuition was completely wrong. Because next she said, "Have you heard of selkies, dear?"

The word was buried somewhere in the recesses of my memory where old stories and childhood books lay.

"I'm not sure," I said.

"Have you seen the seals around here?"

I nodded slowly, remembering that night at the pier. When Princess and I had come face-to-face with a seal.

"Well, selkies. They are—they are creatures of land and sea. It's a rare thing, much like the human being. Proficient in water and out." She spoke rather hurriedly—at least quicker than her normal speech. And her eyes tripped back and forth along the horizon much faster than usual. It was as if she was trying to get the words out before being interrupted. I didn't know what was so special about this story above the others, which always stumbled from her thin lips in slow tangled masses.

"But selkies are slightly different. While humans start on land and learn to navigate water, selkies are born to the water and learn to navigate land. They're creatures that can turn from their seal form to human form at will."

"Is this your … your favorite story?" I asked carefully. I had long been convinced that the old woman believed each of the stories she told. Of course I did not believe in them, but I also didn't want her to know that.

Mrs. O'Leary stopped her rocking chair, and I noticed a glimmer in her eyes. Was it the sparkle of excitement—or the trace of a tear? I couldn't be sure. But she appeared troubled by my question and I felt guilty. I gently prodded her to continue. "So, selkies. They're sea lions?"

She shook her head and recommenced the rocking. "Seals," she corrected.

I nodded. I'd previously thought the two were interchangeable.

"They can shed their sealskins in order to take to the land and live with their human … their human lovers. But only at spring tide. They can only change at spring tide. Beautiful creatures, the selkie women." She touched a crumpled hand to her papery face, and I couldn't help imagining that Mrs. O'Leary would have been a beautiful young woman. Her skin was dark, hinting at a beautiful complexion. And the hair that slipped in wisps out from under her silk scarf was unnaturally dark, even at her age, which I couldn't imagine was any less than seventy-five or eighty.

"The man who captures a selkie, he becomes her husband. But they're usually only in contact for a short time. It is unusual for a selkie to be among humans for a long time. Highly unusual. It is a great love, the one between a human male and a female selkie. *True* love? I don't know. How are we to know that what humans experience is real love?" She paused. "But, Cora, you do remember what I've told you about nature?"

She didn't wait for my answer.

"For all the love in the world, nature abounds tenfold."

Like the Merrow, and her everlasting will to return to the water.

"The selkie will return to the ocean. No matter how strong her love for her human man. No matter how many children she bore him. She needs her sealskin to do so, but when she finds it, she will return to the ocean."

I couldn't shake the feeling that telling me these things was making Mrs. O'Leary nervous. I wished I could relieve her apprehension, but I didn't know what was causing it.

"You know, selkies live much longer than seals or humans," she went on. "And the ones born of a Selkie and her human lover, they age strangely. It is very rare, very, very rare," here, she closed her eyes for what appeared to be a painful moment before continuing, "for a half-selkie offspring to change back to human form after already having returned to nature. But when he takes off the sealskin a second time, the human body is as young as the day he left it."

I was quite at a loss for words, but didn't get the feeling that she was expecting any.

"It is a magical thing, and the seal of the half-selkie will not age again until he is back in the water, just like the human part of him will not age until he walks again on two legs. In seal form, a selkie and her human-born children will age and eventually die, but not for many, many years longer than most things in the ocean. In human form, they would age and die, too, but very few can resist the yearning for the water and live a complete life in human form."

Mrs. O'Leary pressed a hand to her eyes. "Even I don't see like I used to. I was always blind to colors, but now, I need you children to find things. My eyes …"

I didn't know how to console her, but she seemed to snap to rather quickly, and went on unaided.

"Left on land for too long—oh, the selkie will age. Age dreadfully. Eyes that are meant for water, left in the air too long." For some reason this brought the image of the pale, bloated body back to me. Human eyes, left in water too long. For days, weeks.

Mrs. O'Leary finally said, softly, as if defeated, "Thank you for listening."

"I love to listen to your tales," I said. Belatedly, I wondered if she would take offence at the fiction that the word *tale* implied.

"It is nice to speak of this, as I don't tell Ronan this. But everything has a place, even a child knows this."

She doesn't tell Ronan these things? I had heard her on countless occasions speaking of myths and legends to Rory, so I could only wonder if the "Ronan" she was speaking of now was her son, her baby, the dead Ronan O'Leary—or her handyman Rory. Or maybe she did think her son and her handyman were one and the same.

"Nature always wins," the old woman murmured as her rocking chair slowed. Her eyes were drooping, and after a few moments I wondered if she had fallen asleep.

I left her in silence until the sound of a seagull roused her and she was herself again. She launched into a story about Doolin, the town in Ireland where her husband Seamus was born.

Rory appeared at lunchtime. As he climbed the steps with a friendly smile, I could feel my cheeks reacting. I was embarrassed and mad at myself that his mere presence made me have a physical reaction. But the thought of his leggy blonde only made me feel worse, so I sat up straight and willed myself to speak, calmly and as though his presence didn't bother me.

He plopped down on the steps, setting a sandwich on his knee.

"I was just talking to Cora about Ireland," Mrs. O'Leary said.

"Have you been abroad, dear?" she asked me.

I nodded. "My parents go a lot, and sometimes they take me along." *How would Jen answer that?* Radiant and composed, no doubt. I, on the other hand, had cheeks made of tomatoes as I answered and hated myself for it. "I really prefer other places, though," I added, gathering steam from my churning gut. "The less tourist-y countries. You know how commercial and obsessed with tourism a lot of places are becoming."

Rory looked up from his sandwich, and it took me a moment to understand the insult he'd interpreted. Tourism. *Shit. He lives in a resort for Christ's sake!* "Imagine having the luxury to pick your favorite country," he said icily.

"Have you been to Ireland, dear?" Mrs. O'Leary asked me, oblivious of the emotional undertone.

I shook my head, my heart racing. How could I backtrack? Maybe if I pretended I'd never said it. "My parents have never really had a reason to go to Ireland," I said breezily. "They usually travel for my dad's business, but they don't have any factories … or … or offices in Ireland." I trailed off lamely.

"No rainbow shoelaces in Ireland," Rory murmured.

"And where does Princess go when you travel?" Mrs. O'Leary asked, turning the conversation to the dog, per usual.

"She stays at home," I said.

"Poor thing, she must get lonely. Who takes care of her?"

I knew trouble was coming, but I could think of no way to avoid it, and Rory's ignorance of my life only angered me more—so I said it with as much arrogance as I could muster. "The housekeeper watches her," I said.

Sure enough, Rory snorted.

"Someone to keep the house?" Mrs. O'Leary wasn't offending me on purpose. But it was an unfortunate side effect. "What a novel idea. Well, I suppose Ronan is my housekeeper."

"But I would refuse point-blank to be a dog's butler," Rory said.

"Well, yes, but Princess the Beagle is a special dog," Mrs. O'Leary cooed, finding Princess's favorite spot behind the ears. It annoyed me that the old woman was so unwittingly insulting me. "Better to spoil the dog than the children, I would say. It will make for rotten children, but dogs are so good—it couldn't do any real harm to their character."

"So you named her 'Princess' because even your dog is richer than half the country?" Rory mused.

I wanted to yell and perhaps even slap him, if only I could get my wits about me. "No," I said instead. "I named her Princess because when we got her, I was eight years old!"

Apparently any geniality we'd built up was now depleted.

An Leabhar Luachmhar
A VALUABLE BOOK

I SPENT MY JULY EVENINGS WITH OWEN AND company, but my mornings with Mrs. O'Leary. I learned about Seamus O'Leary and all the nuances that the old woman had fallen in love with so many years ago, which she gladly retold like a young woman.

Sometimes Rory was there, sometimes he wasn't. If he was, we would trade snide remarks, Mrs. O'Leary always oblivious. We ignored that slip into decency, maybe even fondness (at least on my part) that belonged to one evening in the past. I was a snob and he always jumped to conclusions about my life. We were too perfectly content, each content with our own imperfect teenage self.

Most days I was there, Mrs. O'Leary would, at some point, ask me to find her jacket. One such day I took the opportunity to delve deeper into the mystery that was this bright yellow house. The living room was, as usual, tidy, though untouched.

For the first time, I walked right through the small entryway, through a low archway, and into the next room. It was darker, but bigger and the walls were also lined with shelves. Here, too, was a giant collection of books. There was a doorway on either side of this room. The one to the left held a closed door, but the one to the right appeared to lead to the kitchen. It was a tiny thing that caused me to shudder slightly. There was a little stove with burn marks on the top and a cream-colored fridge that was probably once white. Not the kind of place Joan would think suitable for preparing a meal.

Before I could venture any farther and maybe find the door to the attic, a small picture frame beside the doorway caught my eye. In the messy organization that was straight book spine after book spine, the old frame looked out of place. There were seashells and bottles of sand and all sorts of things littered about the books, but these were the first photos I had seen.

The frame was long and wooden, with three photos in it. All were of the same young man—standing on the beach with his hands on his hips, sitting proudly in a boat on the beach, arms spread wide, and then sitting in the front of this house. It was her Seamus. The way he sat on the steps and smiled easily at the camera made his face seem familiar to me, as though I had known him myself in some day long past. But what caught my attention was the thing grasped in the young man's hand. It looked suspiciously like my recorders.

I moved back outside to ask Mrs. O'Leary about them, when a book behind the photos caught my eye. It was called *The Selkie Folk*, a big green volume with a dirty spine. This had to be where she got her stories. Maybe I would ask to borrow it. It was heavy, and balancing it on one arm, I cracked it open to flip through.

But to my utter astonishment, it was hollow. The middle of the pages had been carved out and inside there were two stacks of money. The bills were laid flat and neat in the great rectangle cut out from the pages. I stared in disbelief. There were ones, fives, and ten-dollar bills. How much could be in this great, big book?

I looked at the shelves around me that held so many innocent spines. How many were holding such treasure? Surely I hadn't lit upon the only one by chance!

I heard steps from above and gave a great jump, slamming the book shut. Rory appeared in the kitchen from an unseen set of stairs.

Does he know? I thought. *Is that why he helps her?*

"Managed to find her jacket yet?" he muttered, barely pausing to watch what I was doing. "I have been trying for years, you know."

I hastily pushed the book back into its spot on the shelf. It didn't seem as though he knew what it contained. "Nope," I said, following him outside into the sunlight.

"Have I told you about ashrays?" Today Mrs. O'Leary didn't even wait to ask if I'd found her jacket before launching into her own world. I didn't mention that she *had* told me about ashrays before. Instead, I listened obediently. So did Rory. But he was hovering near the stairs, and I was fidgety.

"They say they're these clear creatures that live underwater," Mrs. O'Leary went on. She was talking quickly, as if she could sense that we both wanted to leave and she hoped she could detain us. "You won't find them during the day, they're nocturnal. And they say that when you catch one and expose it to the sunlight, why, it will disappear! And all that's left is a tiny puddle."

"I have to go, Mrs. O'Leary," Rory said. The old woman's face fell, and he seemed sympathetic, but continued his polite excuse. "I promised my mum I'd man the desk for a bit. But I'll be back tomorrow."

She nodded her assent, and he disappeared without acknowledging me.

I left shortly thereafter, too, still full of wonderings. Wonderings about the possibilities of what on earth that woman was preparing her house for. It was very possible that she was simply a lonely old woman wishing to get her affairs and belongings in order before her death. Maybe one of those old-fashioned types that didn't trust banks, kept money under the bed, in the floorboards. But books carved out and filled with bills? That was something you only saw in movies—the stuff of the very stories she spun.

One particularly bright afternoon, I went to town, dragging Owen along at my coattails. I had been meaning to visit the antiques shop on Main Street, but Owen wouldn't leave my sight, so I determined to go regardless of whom or what followed me.

He had offered to drive, and now we walked amicably down Main

Street from the crowded parking lot. The two recorders were in my pocket. As we walked, Owen held my hand and I repeatedly considered pulling away, but it would be more trouble than it was worth. As long as I didn't fall for him again, he was harmless, if not clueless. Owen was in the middle of expounding on some topic I didn't care about when a familiar head of dark hair caught my eye.

Sure enough, walking toward us on the sidewalk was Rory. I had just made up my mind not to be the one to say hello when he noticed me and stopped. "Cora." He seemed to say it out of surprise rather than any actual inclination to talk to me. I *had* appeared on his turf rather suddenly.

I pretended to have just seen him, as if I hadn't been planning to ignore him. "Oh, Rory, hi." He looked at Owen, and then back at me, and I wished with all my might that I would not have to introduce the two.

Rory was looking at me, interested and cocky, with that calculating look. It wouldn't have been so disconcerting if I didn't *still* find his huge brown eyes so incredibly gorgeous.

"I'm Rory," he said, extending his hand to Owen. There was no avoiding it.

"This is Owen," I heard myself say.

"Pleased, I'm sure," Owen said quietly. It was all a blur. A blur of my wishing the three of us were not still standing in the middle of the sidewalk making awkward conversation. A blur of those damn eyes.

"How, uh, how do you two know each other?" Owen finally asked.

I was too confused to respond. "Mutual friend," Rory said, jerking his head vaguely toward the beach. He looked very pleased at my utter lack of composure.

"Cool, well we have to get going," Owen said, not to be outdone by this local boy. I wanted to sound cool and collected, but I had no smart parting words. Instead, I let Owen pull me wordlessly off down the sidewalk.

Just a few storefronts down was the antiques shop. I took a deep breath and forced myself not to look back.

There was a big metal sign that hung over the door of the shop. One of those old-fashioned ones, the red and white paint chipping. It said "Hall's Antiques" in cursive and creaked softly in the wind.

The inside was dim and a bell over the door tinkled as I stepped inside, still dazed from our meeting with Rory. Owen was not exactly happy to be here, but visibly eager to please since the incident at the Ritz party and not about to complain. Disinterested, he hung back and fiddled with rusty metal car parts that filled a big old trunk.

An old man emerged from the back at the sound of the bell. I pulled the recorders from my pocket and walked purposefully to the counter. But before I could say anything, the man spoke.

"How are you doing?" He said it as if he was addressing an old friend, not a new customer. It took me a moment to place him. When I did, I felt all my muscles freeze.

"Fine," I said softly. My hand clenched around the recorders and retracted a bit.

It was the man from the beach, the one with the metal detector. The one that had responded to my screams when I found the body of

Rick Johnson. He was a bit more crouched than I remembered, with very crinkly skin, and his eyes looked especially pained.

"How are you?" I said. It was just to be polite, I didn't want to know the psychological effects that evening had actually had on this old man, but I also didn't want to seem another heartless young hooligan from the big houses.

"I'm doing well, thank you. It was a rough thing to see, though, wasn't it?"

I nodded. My embarrassment might have registered as painful memory, because he looked sympathetic. "I'm sorry to bring it back up," he said. "I hadn't thought you would have known the family."

"I didn't," I said.

He nodded, and there was an awkward silence in which I thought of fleeing the shop. But curiosity about the bloated body of Rick Johnson and his skinny, pretty sister Jen got the better of me.

"Did you?" I said. "Know them, I mean?"

He nodded. "Not the boy personally, but the family runs a great host of businesses in this town. A very big local family."

I questioned myself for a moment, but decided to say it anyway, hoping it wouldn't backfire and that he would tell me more. "I do actually know Jen," I said. "A little."

He nodded. "Wonderfully nice girl. They say she was a great comfort to her mother in the aftermath," he said. "It was a hard thing, several families in the area lost their boys and their fathers, but there's something particularly devastating about such a young man having life cut so short. You know, he was engaged. They were to be married in the winter, as soon as he could be landed for a few days."

A chill went through me as my mind shot immediately to Mrs. O'Leary. How would it be to find the man you truly loved and then to have it be a man who worked at sea? An ever-constant agreement of man and boat. Each does its part—one to carry them safely, the other to guide them home each day. And to be the woman left at home. To wonder every day if the boat would do its part, if he would come home.

Or did she wonder at all? Maybe she never even considered the possibility.

And then one day, they didn't come home. Neither man nor boat.

"The young woman wasn't from here, the fiancée. I hear she's moved away. She was here up until you—until the body was found. Then she moved on."

Mrs. O'Leary; this young woman who fell in love with Jen Johnson's brother. How many others had waited up all night to find in the morning that the boat had failed to bring him home? If you were lucky, some tourist would find the body weeks later. Otherwise, you would spend the remainder of your days, staring at the ocean like Mrs. O'Leary.

Was there a day when you finally stopped believing that he could possibly be alive? *There has to be. But how long does it take?* Three months? A year? Twenty years? I was fairly certain Mrs. O'Leary had never stopped believing.

She still thought Seamus was coming back.

"Of course there were several other poor boys that were on that boat. Two still haven't been found."

I felt a prickling behind my face, and fearful of tears, I recomposed my features and said I had to go.

"I didn't mean to upset you," he said. "But you did come for something?"

I followed his gaze to the recorders I still clutched firmly in my hand. "Yes," I stammered. "I—I was just wondering if you could tell me what these were." The man took the recorders from me and examined them. "Not that I think they're antique or anything, I just didn't know who else to ask. Nobody seems to know what they are."

"Oh, they're tin whistles," he said.

I was taken aback at his easy answer. "What exactly …"

"Have you ever heard Celtic music?" he asked. I shrugged. "Well, they're common in Irish and Scottish music. Very traditional sounding. Where did you get them?"

"I found them on the beach," I said nervously. I felt as though it was admitting to stealing. Which was ridiculous, as I'd seen this very man combing the beach with a metal detector.

"The beach?" he repeated. He looked a little crestfallen. Or perhaps it was confusion, I couldn't be sure.

"Well, I found one up near the big houses and the—"

"The big houses?" he repeated. He was starting to make me uneasy.

"Yes," I said slowly. "Do you know the Ritzes?"

He nodded almost imperceptibly. "I do." He seemed to be thinking very hard.

"Is something wrong?" I asked.

He shook his head quickly, and it seemed to shake the thoughts away. He smiled weakly at me and said, "Is there anything else I can do for you?"

I shook my head and started to back away. "Thanks," I said, motioning for Owen to follow me to the door. "For your help," I clarified stupidly.

"I do want you to know—"

I paused as Owen passed me, out into the sunlight.

"I just want you to know," the old man said again, "I think it was a good thing, how you found the body. Let's that girl get on with her life. *You* helped her to do that."

I was silent.

"There's no sense in it all," he said, "but it makes sense to move on. I think it's a good thing you found that body."

"I think so, too," I said softly.

Bród agus Réamhclaontacht
PRIDE AND PREJUDICE

I DIDN'T MENTION ANYTHING I'D LEARNED ABOUT Jen's family in our subsequent meetings at Mrs. O'Leary's, and Rory didn't say anything about Owen. Not until a day in the middle of July when Mrs. O'Leary asked me to find her jacket. As I was getting up to acquiesce, Rory appeared in the doorway of the house.

"I'll look for it before I leave," he said. It was addressed to Mrs. O'Leary, so I awkwardly returned to my rocking chair.

"Such a darling boy," Mrs. O'Leary said absently. "How I'll suffer when he's gone."

"Mrs. O'Leary," I started awkwardly, remembering the book filled with money. "Are you preparing your house to sell it?"

I expected her to dodge the question, but she didn't. "No, dear, I wouldn't sell this house. It's not my house; it's

Seamus's. I wouldn't sell it without his permission."

I bit my lip. I had heard her talk of him countless times as though he was a long-dead person. But I'd never actually referenced his death in her presence. I wanted to believe she wasn't that unstable. I wanted to believe she wasn't still combing the horizon for his little boat.

"But of course it's yours," I tried. "Through marriage."

The old woman took a shaky breath, her crumpled hands twitching in her lap. "No, it will always be my Seamus's. I just happen to still be stuck here. I'm not inclined to give it away before I must."

"Of course," I said quickly. I didn't want to sound like some young busybody trying to force the old woman into a retirement home or some equally awful place. And in whatever way she seemed to have interpreted my words, they made her nervous. "It was just with all this cleaning up you have Rory … Ronan do. I was just wondering if you were going to be selling it or moving out or something. I know these houses have to be worth a lot, being so close to the ocean."

Rory reappeared then, a navy blue sweater in hand. I had seen him produce this sweater for inspection before. He didn't even seem to wait for her verdict. He slung it over the railing of the porch as she shook her head sadly.

"You seem tired today, Mrs. O'Leary," he said, his eyebrows pushed together in concern. "It's probably time to go inside. I'm finished with the upstairs now. I'll start on the attic tomorrow."

On another day Mrs. O'Leary might have lingered with me on the porch, but she was nervous today and let Rory lead her inside.

"Good night, dear," she said to him at the door.

He closed the front door and let the screen door bang shut, spinning quickly around to face me. "You shouldn't talk to her about the future, it upsets her," he said.

I was taken aback but also extremely put out. She was my friend as much as his. *Well.* Maybe I hadn't known her as long, but she was my friend. "I don't think it concerns you what I talk about with my friend," I sniffed.

"Right, go around upsetting whoever you like," he said. It was on the tip of my tongue to say I hadn't meant to upset her, but he wasn't finished. "It would just be a lot easier for the rest us if you would go upset people on *your* end of the beach. It's kind of crowded down here, and we don't need idle *princesses* hanging around making things harder."

Idle? Princess? I was stung.

"Why don't you go back up to the big houses," he went on. "I know there are more than a few guys with eyes on your money."

Eyes on my money? I was pushed to sputtering: "Is-is it just-just jealousy? Is that what makes you *hate* us so much?"

He snorted. "Yes, I am just driven mad with jealousy for your boyfriend's pink shirts."

"You pretend it's *us* who creates this wall. But it's *you*! I've never heard them say a word against you!" That wasn't entirely true. "Those families have lived here years and years, some probably longer than yours!" I said obstinately. "Those kids, they've been coming here all their lives, too."

"But they don't know what the ocean looks like in the winter," he said simply.

I groaned. "Get off your high horse! You're so stuck atop this pinnacle where you've placed your family and your parents' resort—"

"Yeah, my mom is so unfortunate as to need a job!" he yelled. "I know that automatically puts me some ten to fifteen rungs below you and your nanny."

"I don't have a *nanny*—"

"Oh, that's right. Your dog's the one with the nanny."

"You pretend to know an awful lot about my life," I said, my voice shaking. He snorted again. "But you've been doing that since the day I met you," I barreled on. "Assuming things about me and my life!"

"It's easy to do when you traipse around here like you own the place. Acting like some kind of royalty. Just down south to watch the locals for entertainment."

"I don't *traipse*!" I yelled idiotically. "I come here to visit my *friend*. It's *you* who traipses about, acting like some sort of suffering hero, making stupid assumptions with no interest in correcting them, even when the realities are staring you in the face!"

"Staring me in the face? All that's staring me in the face is a stuck-up, rich kid whose sole occupation for the summer is to walk around the poor side of town talking down to everyone she meets—even her supposed *friends*." He nodded toward the front door, and I could feel the blood rush to my cheeks.

There it was again. But this time it hurt more. Because several things had occurred to me: I thought she was crazy. I thought her kitchen was gross. I hadn't known her name for weeks. I hadn't cared to know her name for weeks; it hadn't mattered to me. Because she was a source of entertainment. Like summer help.

He was right.

The truth brought a stinging to my eyes that I knew preceded tears. I ran down the stairs as fast I could and all the way to my pier without slowing down. It was hard to run in the sand, and I stumbled like a fool, but I didn't dare slow down. There was only one place I felt comfortable crying.

An Finné Fir
THE BEST MAN

I STOPPED GOING TO MRS. O'LEARY'S ALTOGETHER. I didn't want to see Rory. But I also didn't want to see Mrs. O'Leary. I felt as though I had betrayed her. There was nothing left I liked about Oyster Beach.

It was already late July, and it didn't take much for me to convince my parents that it would benefit us all to go home a few weeks early, which was the earliest my mom could get the house together. Dad was rather tired of the social scene and thought it best that we "fix our situation" at home. This meant that when we were home it would be easier for him to contact all his friends to get me into a school he approved of. I knew this, but I didn't resist it. Even that would be preferable to what Oyster Beach had become.

Rory's words had stung me to the core. They were mean, degrading, and offensive. And above all, they were the truth. And that only made me despise Owen and the Carltons and my parents even more.

My mom was sorry to see her perfect world being taken away from her early, but she acquiesced since it would most likely see me to the future she wanted. So Dad set about making plans for the upkeep of the house for the rest of the year. They were going to hire a tenant for the off-season, and Mom happily set about buying the best antiques the area could provide to boost the rental price. We'd be gone by mid-August.

One day, when I returned to the house from a walk along the beach, a walk carefully mapped out to avoid the resort, I found a strange visitor.

Mr. Hall was sitting at our kitchen table, talking to my mother. A huge wave of confusion washed over me—uneasy feelings, thoughts of Jen Johnson, Rick Johnson, Rick Johnson's fiancée, dead, bloated bodies, ashrays. All kinds of eerie things crept upon me with a shiver on my spine.

Mr. Hall nodded a hello as my mom conducted her usual investigation into where I'd been, who I'd been with and what I planned to do next. I shrugged all her questions off, more interested in the quiet old man who inexplicably sat in our kitchen. "What are you guys doing?" I was finally able to ask.

"This is Mr. Hall; he owns an antiques shop in town," she explained.

If he wondered why I didn't correct her assumption about our not knowing each other, he didn't say as much. He had been gone by the time Captain Harville had called my parents that night at the beginning of summer that seemed so far away now. And she, of course, didn't know I'd contacted him about the strange instruments I kept in my pockets.

"I've hired him to look at some of the things in the house," Mom went on. "To see if he can sell any of it. And later he's going to bring over some things that might go nicely with the décor."

"Pink stuff," I mumbled.

Mom rolled her eyes and started talking about lace, so I sneaked around her into the house. But I was restless with a stranger in the house, and later, when I went downstairs, he was the only one in the kitchen. I could hardly turn around and leave the room again without seeming rude, so I made small talk.

"That stuff looks cool," I said lamely.

There were boxes of junk in front of him, boxes with no lids, contents spilling onto the tabletop. He looked at things through a big eyeglass—vases, cups, tablecloths, metal objects with unknown functions—checking them for who-knew-what.

He nodded wordlessly, and I turned to leave the room again, my duty being done, but then he said,

"You talk to Mrs. O'Leary, don't you?"

I stopped. I thought carefully about answering before I turned around and nodded. "How do you know her?" I asked.

"There was a time when everyone in Oyster Beach knew Lia O'Leary."

Lia O'Leary. I had never known her first name. Lia. I had never even considered that a person her age *had* a first name.

I was quiet, but stared at him, willing him to tell me more without my having to ask.

"Seamus O'Leary was my best friend," he said simply.

I sat down at the table across from him.

"I knew Seamus from the day he got to this country."

"Then you knew him when they met," I said. "She's told me before about how they met. And a lot about them when they were younger."

"I told him from the day they met that she was not right for him."

I was appalled. He read my dark expression and added, "They didn't have a happy marriage, you know."

That certainly didn't fit anything Mrs. O'Leary had ever told me. "How so?"

"They were married very quickly after they met. I was the best man." His expression was cheerful for a moment, then flickered back to a dark reminiscence. "Seamus expected people in this town to be happy for him. The town was smaller back then, everyone knew everyone. And he expected them to celebrate his finally settling down. They didn't. He was a loved man, that's for sure. Loved by everybody in this town. Every *woman*, more specifically. He expected them to be just as happy as he was on the occasion. But too many a young lady was conscious of the loss to her own expectations that his marriage produced. And Lia was so pretty. Pretty, but different. So, so different. 'Odd,' people said. 'Strange.' She wore that scarf over her hair, all the time; she looked like a gypsy, they said. Other girls didn't like that. Some wouldn't go near her, wouldn't acknowledge her. But they all, oh, they *all* loved Seamus."

"She loved him, too," I said, instantly on the defense. "You should hear the way she talks about him." I couldn't imagine other women hating Mrs. O'Leary. Or, more accurately, I didn't *want* to imagine it. Because it was only too easy, and too depressing, to see how they would take the eccentric woman and shun her as an outsider. "She still loves him," I said firmly.

Mr. Hall looked at his hands. "That may be true, but it wasn't long after they were married that she was longing to leave. Some loves are stronger than others."

Longing to leave? Mrs. O'Leary was *still* in that dumpy little house. If she wanted to leave, why would she *still* be there?

"You have to understand that Lia was a beautiful woman. Beautiful and … She … And not from around here. Different. She had a dark beauty—long, dark hair, always covered with some colorful scarf. Big, dark eyes. That wasn't the style of women in Oyster Beach. Blonde and sun-bleached was the order of the day. So she stood out. There wasn't a man in Oyster Beach that wasn't taken with Lia O'Leary. Including Seamus. But he always loved her more than she could love him."

"I don't think you're right," I said stubbornly. "She loves him."

"We can agree to disagree," he said simply. He adjusted his glasses and returned his attention to his antiques.

I was not about to let this topic die. "What about the children?" I asked. "Ronan? And the one that died so quickly after being born?"

Mr. Hall looked me in the eye. I got the feeling that he was trying to take the measure of me before going on. I put on my best I-can-keep-a-secret face.

He took a deep breath. "We all thought that would hold her down for a while. After the first baby died—"

"He disappeared," I said. I assumed, being so close to Seamus, that he knew this and was only keeping this from me from years of practiced silence. Or denial. If there was one thing I knew people were good at, it was not telling the whole truth. "I know the baby disappeared," I repeated.

He looked at me with squinted eyes, clearly realizing he had underestimated me. "Okay, disappeared," he finally said. "The doctor was in often to see her after the second pregnancy; she was very ill. Weak. Considered too frail to have children. She was devastated, depressed. Everyone thought it was her inability to have children that depressed her."

I was silent for a long moment. "Who told you that I go to see Mrs. O'Leary?" I finally asked. "Do you go to see her?"

He shook his head. "Bob Harville told me. He's about the only one that goes there these days."

Captain Harville? The cop? I found it odd that the cop would visit her, when even the best friend of Seamus O'Leary wouldn't speak to the poor old widow anymore. But I didn't think that was prudent to say.

He mistook my silence for offense. "Except you, of course," he said.

"And Rory O'Brien," I added.

He nodded slowly. When he spoke again, his voice was brisk and all business; it had lost any hint of the emotion from before. "She's very ill, Lia is. She thinks the O'Brien boy is her son."

"She's lonely," I defended her. "I don't think it's hurting anyone. He doesn't seem to mind."

"Cora, I don't dislike Lia. I feel just as sorry for her as you do. Probably more. I know Seamus is not clear of blame for their trouble. After their son disappeared, Lia was very depressed. And after the second baby, she was in a terrible way. And Seamus used that to his advantage. She was again very eager to leave, but so depressed, it was easier for Seamus to control her. He was protective; he was very afraid she would leave. But it wasn't right for him to trap her there like that."

"Trap her?" I repeated.

Mr. Hall shrugged. "Why guilt her into staying when she wanted to leave?"

I was quiet for a moment. I felt as though Mr. Hall still wasn't telling me everything.

"There's just one thing that doesn't add up," I said. Mr. Hall looked me in the eye, as if challenging me to unravel this story of the O'Learys' which he had bound up so carefully. "If she wanted so much to leave," I went on, "why is she still there in that house?"

Mr. Hall looked down at his hands. "Do you know where your mother is? I need to get back to my shop."

I wanted to run straight to Rory and tell him everything I'd heard from Mr. Hall. He was the only other one who understood this mysterious woman's life. But I couldn't, of course, do that. Instead, I had to content myself with talking to Rosie. But I couldn't tell her about Mr. Hall and Mrs. O'Leary. I felt silly to even have considered it.

She called late that evening with what she deemed "exciting news."

"Just guess what I have to tell you!" Rosie dove right in without even giving me time to express interest in her story. No doubt it would have something to do with Stephen, or the subsequent boyfriend, whatever his name turned out to be. "Just guess!" Of course she didn't really want me to guess. "It's so surprising!" she barreled on. "Guess who asked about you? It shocked me, really! Josh! Josh asked about you!"

I, too, was shocked. My stomach did a quick somersault. Was it joy? I didn't think so. I realized with a great sense of satisfaction that it had actually been many, many weeks since I had thought about Josh Watson.

"Sally Crawford told him you *still* had a crush on him—it's okay, I already yelled at her for it—and so Josh came to me, and, like, asked about you. Like how you were doing and if you were dating anyone. Cora? Why are you being so quiet? Aren't you psyched?"

"Uh, I'm sure you remember the debacle at the movies," I said. "Do you need a refresher?" *Everyone* remembered that day. The day Cora Manchester was humiliated in front of half her friends, half Josh's friends, and several movie-going families.

I remembered everything about that day. I remembered the jean shorts Rosie was wearing when she approached Josh, the soccer player I'd been crushing on for at least a year. "Enough is enough," she had declared, before marching off to do what I wouldn't. To ask Josh

Watson out. *For me.*

I remembered the embarrassed look on Josh's face when he heard Rosie's suggestion. "No, thanks." That's what he'd said. It was worse than "No." It was pity.

I hadn't cried until I'd gotten home. I'd put on a flippant face for everyone, for all of our spectator friends, for Rosie, for my parents. And then I'd climbed into my bed and sunk beneath the covers and cried myself to sleep. Just once. One night. That's all I would give Josh Watson. But it had ached in my soul ever since. That is, until this summer.

"Cora, people can change their minds!" Rosie chirped. "Apparently Josh has!" Her excitement, usually so contagious, wasn't having an effect on me. Something was different.

I started to mumble a protest. I started to say that Josh was just being polite, asking about how I was doing, but I stopped myself. "I don't really care," I said instead.

And this time, it was the truth.

It sang like a glorious songbird inside my chest. I didn't care! I did *not* care about Josh Watson! I didn't care that my friends knew Josh Watson didn't want me. That I wasn't pretty enough or smart enough or popular enough or whatever enough for him. I was *over* it.

"Cora, I know you're like, trying to be all calm, cool and coll—"

"No, Rosie, I'm not," I interrupted. "It's just that I *really* don't care. It's been a long while since I cared about what Josh thought about me."

"Oh." Rosie deflated.

I'm free. This was huge news. I should have been ecstatic. But the songbird inside my chest had already fluttered away. There was one problem. I knew that the reason I hadn't thought about Josh for so long was because I cared a great deal what somebody else thought about me now.

Somebody who had really big brown eyes. Somebody who swam like an Olympian.

Nuair a Casadh an Taoide
WHEN THE TIDE TURNS

IN THE MEANTIME, BARBECUE SEASON WAS IN FULL swing and anniversary parties abounded with the families in the old houses. Apparently every middle-aged couple who summered in Oyster Beach had had a perfect summer wedding.

One such event was a flowery gathering in our own backyard. It was the Carltons' anniversary, and Mom was throwing them a party. It was her first in Oyster Beach (a big day for her) so I was trying to be cooperative. I was wearing my resident fancy dress—the cream-colored one with the big pockets. The only thing I owned that would please my mother. The things Mr. Hall had told me about Mrs. O'Leary had moved me. Disturbed me, to say the least. And so I couldn't help thinking of my own poor mother. I had relegated that dreadful lacey dress to the back of my closet, but my mother had successfully dug it out and implored me to wear it. I did so in order to avoid confrontation and maybe even to please her a little. As if in some way I could alleviate Mrs. O'Leary's past suffering as a mother by being good to my own.

The evening of the party was unseasonably cool, but the backyard was glittering and gorgeous. There were tables and chairs spread around the perimeter with candles flickering to each other in the middle of each table. There were luminaries going down the stairs all the way to the boardwalk. And the back porch was festooned with little paper lights and tables heaped with food and drinks. The caterers had brought servers and they stood around the yard like obedient end tables, balancing trays with ever-replenishing glasses.

And there was to be dancing. A makeshift dance floor had been constructed by the caterers earlier. The band was set up on the landing midway up the stairs.

The guests started to appear at dusk, light summer sweaters and carefully wrapped presents under their arms. It was picture-perfect, and my mother was beaming.

"Thank you," she said unexpectedly. I was standing next to her at the top of the stairs. Dad was at the bottom, greeting the Ritzes and another family, whose name I couldn't remember.

"For what?" I asked.

She grasped my arm with one hand and held out the skirt of my dress in the other. "For being my daughter," she said. She kissed me on the forehead and then rubbed the lipstick off with her thumb. There were tears in her eyes as she floated down the stairs. My stomach fell a few feet. Why was it always so difficult for me to just *be* her daughter?

She only has one. And not by choice.

I was always angry at her for not talking to me about these things, about the big things, about why we were here this summer, why she couldn't let me make my own decisions about the rest of my life. But the truth was that she was always talking, *always*, I just didn't want to listen.

The party was a smash hit, but I tired of it quickly. I managed to stand near the stairs with a look of silent amusement on my face, hopefully masking my disdain inside. All I thought about was Mrs. O'Leary. Or more accurately, Rory. And about how right he was. About everything he'd said. I even looked down on my own mother.

I wondered what Mrs. O'Leary would say if she saw these people in our backyard. Would she tell them her stories? *Would they make fun of her?* Surely Blondie would call her a crazy old bat. But these thoughts distressed me more because I knew it wasn't Mrs. O'Leary I was thinking of. Not really. It was Rory, what he thought of me, what he would think of this scene. And that just proved his point. Even when I thought I had the old woman's interests in mind, they were purely selfish ones.

Not wanting to be a part of the good-byes, I made my way toward the beach when the crowd started to thin. The couples were saying their drunken good-byes to the Carltons and my parents, while kids sneaked away, grasping the hand of the opposite sex, or perhaps an armful of beers.

I laughed at the wine in my own hand. I didn't even like wine. But I disliked it less than beer, so I had grabbed it from one of the servers. If only to stop the constant badgering, from guests and servers alike, to have a drink. And then I had grabbed another. And another. And who knows how many others.

Maybe I was drunk or maybe it was just my annoyance at seeing Owen approach, but I started to laugh.

"What's so funny?" he asked, as he joined me on the beach.

I slipped off my shoes and ran to the soft sand left wet by the ebb tide. It was freezing cold, but I plunged into the water until the waves were up to my knees.

Owen hesitated at the edge of the water. "You're drunk," he said with a laugh.

Maybe I was. That could certainly be the ticket to stomaching life in the big houses. No wonder they guzzled wine and cocktails at an alarming rate. But I just shook my head with a laugh. "I'm not drunk. I'm just looking for Shoney."

"For what?" he asked.

"The ale-loving water spirit," I said simply.

"Is this another one of those stupid stories you got from that crazy old lady?"

Before, that statement might have made me angry. I would have told him he was an ignorant, arrogant ass. But it didn't hurt now. Because I regarded it as mere evidence of a truth. A truth about him. A truth about me. A once-painful truth. But now there was a scar where it hit, and it merely bounced off painlessly. "Yes, it is," I said. I swirled the wine around the glass and watched some of it slop over the side.

"You've gone insane," Owen said. "She's rubbed right off on you."

For some reason, at this, I cackled. "Shoney! Shen-en-an-doya-ya. Shoney, I present to you this wine so that thou—" Here, I hiccupped. "Thou will send us good … good harvest for the coming … the coming harvest."

"Wasted," Owen muttered.

"Imagine," I was saying, "someone so easily"—hiccup—"pacified."

"That's about all it takes for me," Owen said.

"It's supposed to be ale," I said. "But I don't know where to find that."

That's when we heard the shouts drifting down from the house. Angry, drunken shouts.

"Time to go, drunkie," Owen said, holding his hand out to me. I let him lead me back up to the house, carrying our shoes, but Mrs. Carlton met us on the boardwalk in a huff.

"Come on, Owen, we're going home!" she said, her eyes throwing daggers in my direction.

"Mom—"

"Get away from that *tramp*, let's go!" In shock, Owen let his mother pull him away north and off down the boardwalk. Striding past me, Mr. Carlton averted his eyes, his mouth a thin line.

My dad appeared beside me. He put a hand on my shoulder.

"Did I do some"—hiccup—"thing?"

He sighed and shook his head.

"I'm not getting inta St. Bernard—ammi?"

He just shook his head again and went about setting the remaining guests on their way home.

Inside the house, my mother was standing at the kitchen counter, Princess hovering at her feet, carefully hopeful eyes on the servers who moved about, washing dishes and packing away rented plates and uneaten food. Mom watched them with glowering eyes.

I didn't know whether or not to broach the topic, but I finally decided on a peaceful, "How are you, Mom?"

"For God's sake, Cora, let's not talk about it in here," she said. Her eyes flashed around the room and she stalked into the empty living room. Princess was at her heels and I followed reluctantly. Of course she didn't want to fight in front of the hired help, but I had the nagging feeling that this was about me—and I would have liked witnesses there in case she was in the mood for murder.

In the living room she sat down. I could see there were tears in her eyes.

"Did something happen to Mrs. Carlton?" I asked lamely. I tried to stifle a hiccup.

"That insolent witch had one too many drinks is what happened," she said severely. I saw her wipe her eyes.

"She called me a tramp," I said quietly.

"She called you a lot worse than that," Mom said. I turned red. I couldn't tell if I was the victim here or the guilty party. "She has no right, no *right*, to come into *my* house and talk like that about *my* daughter. There's a lot worse that can be said for her dumpy little dud of a girl."

I couldn't stifle the grin on my lips. So I was to be defended. "What exactly did she think I had done?" I asked carefully.

"Oh, nothing more than is true!" she flashed suddenly. *Uh-oh.* "You spending all your time over there in that—that *place* with all those locals and the *motel.* That's what you're doing! Shunning every kid, every respectable person we put in front of you. Acting so proud and above everyone here!"

"*Proud?* Shunning *who?*" I demanded. "Wasn't I just down there letting Owen Carlton make ridiculous puppy eyes at me?"

"As if the whole world can't see you running around with those people like a regular … well, a *tramp!*"

"What are you talking about?" I sputtered. "Why—Why in the world did you defend me? Why did you stick up for me if you agreed? Why let something as ridiculous and superfluous as your daughter come between you and your *precious* Linda Carlton!"

"Yes, yes, turn this around on *me.* I'm the bad guy here." She stood and grabbed a handful of seashells that I had stowed on the end table by the couch. "I've spoiled you," she said, holding up the shells, as if they were evidence. "That's what it is. I've let you have the run of the world! It's time to shape up, Cora."

"That's lofty, coming from someone who had to be taught laundry by a housekeeper at the age of fifty-two."

"Yes, well, luckily you won't come to that! From here on out, you're doing your own laundry, emptying your own goddamn pockets—" She threw the seashells back on the table with a clatter. "And for Christ's sake, in one month, you're going to whatever college I pick out!"

I cried myself to sleep in my lacey dress that night and still felt like crying when I woke up. I couldn't remember a time in my life when I'd cried this much. I hadn't been to Mrs. O'Leary's since my fight with Rory, but I didn't know where else to go. Sure I could go and cry at the pier, but the truth was, I missed Mrs. O'Leary. Actually missed her, and nobody, not even Rory, could convince me otherwise. A purely selfish motive, I wanted to hear her soothing voice and feel better.

But what would I say after being away so long? I grabbed the tin whistles and stuffed them in the big oversize pockets on the front of my dress, a good cover motive. If Rory didn't want me talking to her about the future, I would talk about the past. And Seamus definitely knew about these little instruments. I would talk about *anything* to get my mind away from the Pink Palace.

I scraped my tangled hair into a bun and pulled a sweatshirt on over my dress, then shuffled off to her house before my parents woke up.

But when I saw her on the porch, I quickly forgot about any of my planned conversation. I even fleetingly forgot why I was upset.

She sat on the porch, rocking slowly, in the same position as usual, but her face was stony and her eyes watery. She'd mentioned on numerous occasions that her eyesight was failing.

Her face opened in surprise when she saw me. "You haven't been around in a while," she chirped. It was feigned cheerfulness.

"I know, I'm sorry," I said. I briefly considered telling her about

Rory's words, with some amendments of course, but I didn't want her to tell me they weren't true. I knew they were.

"Oh, no need for apologies," she said. "I know I'm just an old woman; I just missed your burst of energy every day, that's all." I knew it was a sad state of affairs for someone to consider *me* a high point of their day. I filled with pity and remorse that she had been able to say what I had not—that I considered her a friend. This filled me with such a fond feeling, I wanted nothing more than to pour my aching heart out to her.

"Have you heard of kappas, dear?"

I shook my head slowly and sat down tentatively on my rocking chair. But I didn't want to get caught up in another story. Today, *I* wanted to do the talking.

"They say there are these creatures in the water, they have green skin supposedly, and they pull children down. Drown them."

The lump was back in my throat. I gulped it down quickly. "Mrs. O'Leary," I said valiantly. "I need to talk to you. I had a fight with my mom, and then I realized you're the only other person I can talk to about it."

Mrs. O'Leary's eyes were pulled from the horizon and landed on me. They were shifty and looked nervous, but her voice was even as she returned her gaze to the ocean. "Yes, of course, dear, what is it?"

"My mom ..." I was editing the story in my head; I didn't want her to know that my own mother was disapproving of the south end of the beach and, most probably, Mrs. O'Leary herself. "My mom isn't proud of me," I finally said. "She complains all the time. But then last night she yelled at someone that criticized me."

Mrs. O'Leary didn't seem to understand.

"It's just that I feel as though she hates who I am, but then she goes and does something to make me think she is the tiniest bit … well, proud." I was definitely grasping at straws now. Words were coming out quicker than their corresponding thoughts could form in my head. "I can't tell if she's ashamed or proud, and I get the feeling that she doesn't know either. I feel like I'm living this pre-arranged life where she's running along a little in front of me, trying to set everything up as we go, but she keeps stumbling. And so then I keep stumbling."

I took a deep breath.

"I had a sister," I said. "Only it doesn't feel right to call her my sister. She died before I was born. She drowned. So I never knew her. She's just this vague idea that made a lot of people sad in the past, but nobody talks about anymore. That whole thing spawned this huge, irrational fear of the water that, like, runs in our family."

I had been holding my breath and it was coming out fast, in my words. "And, so, I guess sometimes I feel like maybe my mom is so focused on doing everything right this time, and just, gets it wrong." I finished up shakily, leaving my own self rather confused.

"Dear, I do not know the circumstances, but I assure you that every mother feels the tiniest bit of pride in her child, no matter how much time goes by. But what you have to remember is that losing a child, for a mother, is a pain like no other."

My body filled with regret. Rory was right yet again. There I was thinking only of myself. How could I have been so callous as to bring up something as sensitive as children to Mrs. O'Leary? Everything Mr. Hall had said about her depression after her children's deaths, her troubled marriage, it all came flooding back to me. I was making her relive all that pain.

I was about to change the subject when she knocked me out of all reservations.

"Ronan is a good example."

"What?" I said.

"I think of Ronan and I am more proud of him than anyone else in the world. I don't think it would matter if he killed someone; it wouldn't lessen my pride."

I wasn't sure if we were talking about Ronan O'Leary or Rory.

"Maybe your mother is disappointed that you are not like her or like her first child," she said philosophically. "But I assure you that doesn't change how much she loves you, takes pride in you, despite herself."

I had forgotten my own mother now. Every word she said I saw as a comment on her own children, or on the local boy she *thought* was one of her children.

"I sometimes wonder about kappas, and what must it be like for the human mother that never sees her child return from the ocean. Your poor, poor mother. She must know."

Wonder? But her own children had drowned. Or … or *something*. She couldn't possibly believe her children were still alive? Was she still waiting for Seamus *and* her children?

Rory had said not to speak to her of the future. I realized then that this was because she was still so firmly entrenched in the past. "It must be similar to the wife who doesn't see her husband come home," I said softly.

But she shook her head. "A grown man is something different. You trust a grown man. But a child." She paused. "I don't know what I'll do when Ronan leaves."

I was silent.

"I will miss that boy so much," she said.

I was completely lost. I didn't want to confuse her, upset her. But at the same time, the mere mention of the boy brought weird twisting feelings to my stomach. And it wasn't just because it made me question Mrs. O'Leary's state of mind.

Despite what I tried to tell myself, I had the distinct impression that what I felt when she referenced Rory were the pangs of *missing* someone. Despite his mood swings and his inability to decide whether he hated me or found me slightly amusing, he made me laugh, he made Mrs. O'Leary laugh. I just couldn't figure out who he was. The problem was that Mrs. O'Leary had a way of painting a portrait of this complicated person that was quite impossible not to fall for. Was he the cynical, aloof boy who thought I was a snob—or was he the kind, caring Rory that Mrs. O'Leary loved and that I'd gotten a few glimpses of myself?

Mrs. O'Leary shifted her feet on the floor. "Cora, I'm ready to go now," she said quite softly. For the first time, the shock of her dark hair hit me with full force. How utterly out of place it was. I had no idea of her age, but the wrinkles on her face hinted that her hair should have gone gray decades ago. Her face was crinkly as sandpaper. But her hair, it was every bit as dark as mine. It was quite unnatural. Surely she wasn't one to dye her hair. "Yes, I'm ready to go," she repeated.

"Inside?" I tried to clarify.

"No!" she said severely. "When that boy leaves, I'll have no hope left! I'm ready to go *now*." It was the sternest I'd ever heard her speak. She sounded frightened. And that frightened me.

"Mrs. O'Leary, I can help you," I said. "What if I stayed when the summer is over and helped you?"

The old woman took a deep, withering breath from the depths of her tiny body and let it out slowly through her thin lips. "Just children," she murmured. "They were just children." Her eyelids fluttered and settled at half mast. "Why did they get to go when I want to so badly?"

To Ireland? Or was she talking about Seamus? Or her babies? Or were they just the mad ramblings of a woman slowing, meticulously losing her grasp on reality?

I didn't want to leave her, but I also didn't want to continue this conversation. It seemed to be draining the life right out of her. Suddenly, I remembered the tin whistles in my pocket.

"Mrs. O'Leary, do you know what these are?"

Her eyelids fluttered up for a fraction of a second to gaze at my palm. "Those are tin whistles," she said simply. I pretended not to have known this and feigned happiness at the answer. "My Seamus could play." Of course, I had surmised as much from the photo, but I again pretended to be surprised. "You know, Ronan can play, too."

I hadn't known that. I also no longer had any idea who she meant when she used that name.

"My Seamus gave him lessons right here on this porch. Ronan loved to set people to dancing in the middle of the day just by picking up a tin whistle."

Assuming her child would have been too young at the time of his death, I realized with a strange twist of my stomach that she must have meant her Seamus had taught young Rory O'Brien to play the tin whistle.

"I'm so ready to go, Cora," Mrs. O'Leary said again. "He's not coming back." Her eyes roved the ocean.

Not knowing what to say to calm her nerves, I merely put my hand on top of hers, which lay limp on the arm of the rocking chair. It was dry and papery, a bumpy map of veins and knots. She didn't react to the touch. Her eyes continued to rove the horizon and her feet continued to rock the chair ever so gently.

We stayed like that until the sun began to set, and she was ready to go inside.

Mapa agus Urlár Salach
A MOP AND A DIRTY FLOOR

A S THE LIFE IN THE BIG HOUSES BECAME MORE and more repulsive to me, my mother's sulkiness festered, and my concern for Mrs. O'Leary heightened, I began to spend all day with the little old woman again. She seemed to be growing more and more restless as the summer waned, so I steered conversation carefully away from sensitive material. And I grew more certain that she wasn't well.

One day at the beginning of August, as my days in Oyster Beach dwindled, Mrs. O'Leary asked me to run to the Resort to get Ronan. She said, out of nowhere, that the toaster was broken and needed immediate fixing.

I suggested I look at it, but she insisted Ronan be fetched. Regardless of not wanting to face him, I had tender feelings toward the old woman what with our recent talks and the way her eyes had begun to hold a watery fearfulness. Rory's painful reproach of my behavior toward Mrs. O'Leary still burned, but despite the way my stomach turned over, I feigned cheerfulness and agreed to go get him.

"You just go to the main office, the big red building, and Mr. or Mrs. O'Brien will be there, and just ask for Ronan."

I nodded and told Princess to "stay" before walking off down the boardwalk.

Make your peace, I told myself sternly. I was determined to take advantage of this situation and change the way this boy thought of me. Show him I had changed.

The big, red, two-story cabin looked deserted from outside, but I went in anyway. A bell tinkled overhead as I entered, and a woman popped up from behind the desk quite unexpectedly.

I must have started because she laughed heartily. "I'm sorry, pet," she said. "I was fetching a pencil, though I do seem to have lost it for good." She was short and squat with a round, rosy face, but all this was barely noticeable under her strong Irish accent. I assumed this was a relative of Rory's, but I couldn't put my finger on any particular resemblance. "What kin I do for yas?"

"I'm looking for"—I paused here and bit back the name Ronan—"Rory."

She smiled but looked confused. "You a friend a his from school?"

"No, I'm a friend of Mrs. O'Leary's," I said.

"Oh, dear child, you must be the girl from the big houses." She was absolutely beaming as she came out from behind the front counter and beckoned for me to follow her. "I'm Rory's mum."

"Cora," I said, shaking her hand. I was more than surprised to hear such an accurate guess of my identity. *What has he said about me?* Or had she been talking to Mrs. O'Leary?

She led me down a narrow hallway. It was brightly lit and covered with pictures of children at various ages. The woman walked rather slowly and I studied them for the familiar face as I passed.

"Your family here for the summer?" the woman asked, occasionally darting interested glances over her shoulder. She seemed pleased with the interest I took in the pictures on the wall. "Won't find Rory in many of these pictures, sweetheart," she said. "Always in the water, that lad, rarely in front of the camera."

"He swims a lot," I said, a half-question. I felt braver under the guise of friendship that his mother assumed we had.

She laughed loudly. "That's an understatement, child. The boy lived in water till 'e was five. 'e was devastated to learn that school for human lads wasn't quite like schools of fish. Still swims every mor'n fer hours." She paused for a moment and then went on. "I suppose you've heard Mrs. O'Leary call 'im Ronan."

I nodded.

"That name, it means 'little seal.' I'n't the strangest? This boy spends more time in the water than out. And there's little Mrs. O'Leary, calling 'im the wrong name that means 'little seal.'"

She stopped and pointed to a picture above both our heads. "There 'e is, just a tot." It was a picture of a smiling kid in water wings and up to his neck in the ocean. Looking closer, it did look a lot like the Rory I knew.

"You have other sons?" I asked.

"Gracious, child, we've five others. Rory's the youngest but one."

"Five?" I repeated. The woman's smiling red face had lulled me out of my temerity and I looked openly around at the pictures now.

"Our four oldest boys"—she indicated a picture of a mob of smiling boys all with very similar faces—"and my two girls were born in Ireland, then Rory and Aidan joined us after we'd settled down in Oyster Beach."

"They all look so much alike," I said.

A little crease appeared between Mrs. O'Brien's eyes, but she didn't say anything. I went back to scanning the pictures. It was a moment before I realized she was walking away down the hall. I skipped to catch up with her.

"Rory's doing rounds now," she went on, "we've a big party coming up at the weekend, and we'll all be running around with our heads cut off then, but for now he should be easy enough to track down."

"Oh, if he's busy, I'm sure—"

"Nonsense, child, if Mrs. O'Leary is wanting 'im, he best go. But if ya'd be good enough and take something down to 'im fer me." We emerged into a sort of backyard where a lone boy was watering plants with a hose at the side of a patio.

"Aidan, where's yer brother got'oo?" Mrs. O'Brien called across the yard.

The boy looked up and sure enough it was a miniature version of Rory, brown eyes and all. He had a messy mop of dark hair that fell just a little longer than Rory's. Brushing the back of his hand across his forehead to push stray strands out of his eyes, he cast me a furtive, curious glance.

"He's down by ten," he said, with much the same voice as his brother.

"Alright, child"—Mrs. O'Brien turned back to me—"I need to get back to the desk, but if i's alright with ya, I'll send ya that way an' if ya could take this"—she retrieved a mop and bucket from beside the door from which we'd just emerged—"he'll know what to do with it," she finished with a smile.

"Sure thing," I said. I was vaguely aware of Aidan's curious gaze, and I tried my best to keep my composure. "Thank you so much."

"Just follow this walk down and the cabin numbers will rise, and 'e should be right near cabin ten." Mrs. O'Brien motioned toward a smaller version of the boardwalk, and after more profuse thanks, I scampered away.

The path wound past and between the red cabins, none of which seemed too occupied. They were small and most of them were on stilts, occasionally interspersed with small white houses that must have been privately owned. The boardwalk grew skinnier as it went on, and my nerves grew weaker as I wandered down it. The inevitable awkwardness of the situation was just making itself utterly apparent when I reached cabin number ten. But there was nobody in sight.

A little relieved, I decided to walk to number twelve before giving up, for Mrs. O'Leary's sake, but he was nowhere in sight. I turned around to go back.

"Cora?"

Damn! So close.

"What are you doing here?"

I spun around to see him emerging from the side of the cabin, clutching a large bulging trash bag. He looked just as startled as I felt. His hair was messed up and sweaty around his ears, but that didn't stop my heart from pounding a little quicker than normal. His face was flushed and at this point in time, his brown eyes looked nervous.

"I come bearing gifts," I said, lifting up the mop and pail with a weak smile.

He was resentful. "I'm really sorry."

"No, what? No, it's fine," I sputtered. *Be friendly. Make him like you. And,* cheeks, *you behave!*

"God, did my mum put you up to that?" He put the trash bag down and hurriedly went to take the mop and bucket from me. For the slightest second, I thought I heard the twinge of an accent in his words, and I smiled.

"I know what you think of me, thanks to a profusion of very strong words, but I *do* know how to work a mop," I said. *Good. Keep going.* I let him take the bucket but held firm to the mop. "Not from practice, of course, but I've studied Joan for eighteen years, and I'm a great student." It took all of my strength to will a self-deprecating smile from the depths of my being. "That's the housekeeper," I added. I hoped he would understand the peace offering I was trying to make. When it came down to it, it was an admission that he was right, that he'd seen me correctly, that I was trying to change.

But these were thoughts too complicated for the few seconds it took for him to smile back and then laugh, and I felt a simple flooding of relief. He was rubbing his head with one hand, much like I'd just seen his brother Aidan do, and looking at me confusedly.

"Mrs. O'Leary sent me to get you," I said, again blabbering in the silence. "But now I'm on a serious mission from a Mrs. O'Brien. Do you need help?"

He licked his lips absentmindedly and looked around him a little bashfully. Was he—I ventured to imagine it—embarrassed?

"Seriously, it's probably time I did some fieldwork," I added.

He finally rummaged in his pocket and pulled out a ring full of keys. His eyebrows were pushed up and together, and he looked at me out from under a creased forehead, as though unsure of what he was doing.

"It's no Pink Palace," he said, as I followed him into cabin twelve, smiling with the glee Rosie would undoubtedly feel when I told her I'd been alone in a resort cabin with a boy. Granted, romance was usually much easier when said boy didn't have a history of loathing you and gallivanting with pretty blonde girls.

The room was a cozy, dark thing with stone walls and floors. There was a small kitchen area with a long table and couches around the perimeter. It was decorated like a country home, pastoral scenes framed and hung on the walls and cozy floral prints on all the furniture. *Tacky,* my mother would have called it. Rory filled the bucket at the sink and set it on the floor, then held his hand out for the mop.

I smirked and dipped the mop into the bucket. I attempted a weak imitation of Joan (though I'd said it in jest, I really never had mopped before), slapping the wet mop across the floor in random arcs and leaving streams of water on the floor. I looked up to find him leaning back against the fridge, arms crossed across his chest, looking at me with amusement, and something else, which I dared to hope was somewhere along the lines of satisfaction.

He came forward and took the mop from me. His big hands brushed mine and I tried to hide the quick change in my breathing. He motioned for me to go sit on the nearby couch. "I think you need to study a little longer before going into the business," he said, wringing out the excess water in the mop back into the bucket.

"I'm just not used to such an ancient piece of technology," I said playfully. "You should invest in a Swiffer." *Too soon to joke about money?* I wondered.

"Ah, that's an investment beyond our means," he said. I flooded with relief. Apparently we were on to the stage where we could joke about it. "It's a meager living, this place, and, alas, we're destined to mop until the end of our days."

It was such a simple difference, but he worked the mop with long, deliberate strokes. The mopping of a kid who'd done it before—been doing it all his life, perhaps.

"It sounds as though you won't be," I said after a slight hesitation. Though joking was a big step, I wasn't sure we'd quite gotten to the point where a serious conversation could be had. Perhaps he was only hiding his distaste for me behind his playful sarcastic comments. Perhaps he still detested me as much as ever. But I was quite beyond any feelings of that kind.

"What's that?" he said.

"Don't you go to Ireland soon?"

"August thirtieth," he said. He jabbed the mop back and forth across the floor, and I vacantly watched his forearms twist and bulge with the motion. It made my stomach flutter.

"Are you going to school there?" I asked.

"Dunno. Probably. And work. Until I get on my feet."

"Get on your feet?" I repeated. "Does that mean you're *staying* there?"

He laughed. "Yeah."

"For good?"

"That's the idea."

This was a foreign idea to me. There were semesters abroad and there were years spent travelling and there were business trips. But up and moving across the globe didn't happen. Not in my world.

He noticed my silence and looked up. "That's weird to you?"

I shrugged. "You know, Mrs. O'Leary is going to miss you."

"Yeah, but there are plenty of people to take care of her here. I'll set Aidan on the house, for one thing. Once she gets used to it, she'll be happy. It's what Seamus always wanted."

"To go back to Ireland?" I asked.

He nodded. "That's why some people think it was suicide."

He couldn't have committed suicide. *He loved her.* That's what Mr. Hall said.

"I'm no great authority, but I don't think it was," he said. "A suicide, I mean. He was a happy man. They all yearn for going back some day, but he had a greater happiness here. With her."

"Nature," I breathed softly.

"What?"

"Mrs. O'Leary told me once that nature overcomes everything. That everything has a place. Everything goes back to nature. Is your natural place in Ireland?"

He shrugged and started mopping again. "I guess I don't know yet. I'm an American citizen, so I guess, legally, my place is here. But my older brothers and sisters were born there. They say my parents were Irish, too."

I tried to hide my confusion. His mother's accent was rather obvious. He smiled. "I was adopted," he explained easily.

"Oh." *Adopted?* This boy was a giant question mark. What else didn't I know about him? The silence was uncomfortable, and I didn't want him to know all I was wondering about his life. "You won't be lonely over there?" I asked quickly.

"I have three brothers there. That's more than I've got here. I've got seven nieces and nephews, too, and they're growing up entirely too fast. And sisters-in-law and cousins, too many cousins to count." He'd stopped mopping and was just talking passionately while leaning on the mop handle. "And a bachelor of a brother willing to put me up. I've got to go before he decides to get married and I'm out of a free room."

"Have you been to Ireland before?"

"Some of us go back every year for Christmas. Not all of us, every year. It's really expensive. But as many as can go each year. And then my brothers, they have childhood friends there, they started moving back as soon as they could afford it. Two of them went to college there, and never left."

"So you've got a winter home, too," I said quietly.

He looked me in the eye for a long moment and then smiled. "I guess you could say that."

It was quiet again and it made me uncomfortable. So I babbled. "Of course, if I had the means, I'd get out of here, too," I said. "I mean, away from home. Not *here* here."

He smiled. "*You* not having the means? Is it strange that I found that a bit of an oxymoron?"

I shook my head. "I think that's one thing that you never understood." I was careful, broaching the subject of the fight on tiptoe. "It isn't my money. It's money for me, on one condition. On the condition that I make the decisions that they want me to make. Sort of a farce, I guess. Pretend to make the decisions, while they call the shots, then sure, I've got means." I trailed off, but he had no response. "But you, you seem to have it good. Why would you want to leave?"

He was quiet for a moment. "I guess I am lucky in that respect. I've always had the freedom to do what I want with my minimum wage. I guess this would sound strange to you, but this place has never felt like home. I've lived here my whole life. But in Galway every year, going back there, it just feels like home." His face was contorted in a familiar way that I'd seen him use in my presence before, as though he was trying to work out a difficult equation. "What's home but where your family is?" he went on. "I mean, the family I was raised with. And so much of my family's there. Really, what's home but where the people who love you reside? And my mum and dad become so much more *themselves* there. I don't know if that makes sense."

Strangely, it did to me. In so many different ways. Not least of all with my own father.

"Well, Mrs. O'Leary will miss you," I said quietly. "Oh *God*, Mrs. O'Leary!" I stood and moved toward the door. "She'll want you to go see her when you can. I need to go say good-bye to her for the day, I need to get home." My cheeks were red, and for some reason I suddenly felt the need to be away from this boy whose mere presence made me so nervous.

"Home? Where's home?" he said playfully.

I smiled in spite of myself. "Well, I meant the Pink Palace, if home is where your family is. But I'm not sure I buy your definition of home."

"Oh, really? And what definition do you *buy*?"

"Well, honestly … I don't think I'm old enough to know yet." I waved awkwardly and left, wondering where in that conversation my stomach had started doing mad somersaults.

Lúnasa
LUGHNASADH

IT WAS THE FIRST WEEKEND IN AUGUST. OWEN AND company were becoming antsy with the waning summer, and they were all eager for entertainment. Unfortunately, we had different ideas of what constituted entertainment.

"It's some sort of party for locals," Blondie explained. "It happens every year, but we've never been before."

"We're not locals," I pointed out.

I knew the only reason the kids from the big houses wanted to go was because their parents would be appalled if they found out. Forbid a person to do something and it becomes substantially more inviting, I knew this from firsthand experience. This, however, was something I really didn't want to do.

"The locals don't care, they'll all be drunk anyway," Owen said.

"I don't want to crash a party," I said.

"We're not crashing."

"Oh, *I* want to crash a party!" the bimbo squealed. "I've never crashed anything before!"

Owen rolled his eyes. "Cora, it's a party. If it was private there wouldn't be signs plastered over half the town." I didn't trust Owen like I once had, I'd learned my lesson. But my mother's recent accusation of shunning these kids was fresh in my mind. If it would keep all parties involved placated, maybe it was worth it.

I reluctantly agreed.

"Sweet, let's go drink their beer," Benjamin Huston said.

The night of the party was hot. My balcony doors were flung open, but there was no wind. I had been on the phone with Rosie when I heard Owen downstairs. It was rare that his voice brought relief, but Rosie's conversation was waxing difficult.

"I'll call you later, Rosie," I said, interrupting a rather long account of her latest date with Steven.

"Oh—uh, ok."

Why on Earth are you surprised nobody wants to listen to this boring story? Rosie's constant need to validate her existence with the attention of guys our age was becoming more and more annoying to me as the summer wore on. At least that's what I told myself. In reality, it felt very similar to jealousy.

I hung up and slipped into my one-and-only lacey party dress. It was still slung over the trunk at the bottom of my bed; apparently my mother's flippant resolution not to do my laundry still held firm.

I glanced in the mirror and greeted my reflection with a grimace. Rosie would have started preparing for an event like this hours ago, makeup spilling over her desk, straightener and curler both out, plugged in, and threatening to burn the house down. But I was another story. Any attempt to tame my hair or skin only resulted in my looking a bit like a clown. *Better to look like a hobo than look like you're trying too hard*, I thought. My stomach curled with the desire to look like Rosie did at the end of her preparations, primped and perfect. But it was really a fear of failure that kept me from pulling out my ancient stash of makeup. *You can't fail if you don't try.*

Downstairs, Owen was positively glowing as he chattered to my father. He wore khakis and a soft white shirt unbuttoned nearly to his belly button. Never had he been more the personification of Abercrombie. He talked easily with my dad, at home in the big kitchen. My mother stood idly by, saying nothing for the first time in her life, and merely nodding as we left. I wasn't sure if the silent treatment was meant for me or for the odious Linda Carlton's son, but I had a feeling Mom didn't know either.

Outside, Blondie and the bimbo simpered over my dress, obviously having forgotten they'd seen it a dozen times before. The Huston kid was already drunk. Even Marshall Ritz was there, eyes glazed. *Did they invite the whole neighborhood?* There was no way we could inconspicuously crash a party where the locals would undoubtedly know everyone else.

Including me. Because that was the real problem, wasn't it? What would the kids from the big houses think if we came across some Oyster Beach local who knew me?

But my misgivings didn't really become uncontrollable until we began to near Mrs. O'Leary's little yellow house. "Hey, where is this thing?" I asked Owen, feigning nonchalance.

"I don't really know; somewhere in back of a motel," he said.

There was only one place that could be misconstrued as a motel. My stomach dropped.

"I'm really reconsidering this," I said quickly. "I think it's a bad idea."

Owen rolled his eyes. "I don't know why you're being so weird," he said. "We're not dealing crack or something."

"Benjamin's already drunk." I was grasping at anything. "He's just going to start a fight or something."

"Jesus, Cora, no he won't. This isn't *West Side Story.*" He was right; Benjamin was a Huston, he'd probably never used his knuckles in his entire life. Desperation to be anywhere but here was flooding my veins.

Unfortunately, we didn't have to search for the party. The resort was backlit and awash in chatter and music. People were flocking to the patio behind the office.

The first person I saw was none other than Aidan O'Brien.

Shit.

He stood at the side of the building, talking brightly to some younger girl. He was the spitting image of his brother. Aidan might let me pass unnoticed, but if I knew Rory (and I liked to pretend I did) he would say hello. He was so goddamn *sweet*.

What on Earth would I say to him?

Hey, what are you doing here? Oh, is this your parents' resort? I didn't even notice!

Shit. Shit. Shit.

Hey, Rory! I'm just here at your party. It's open to the public, right?

I followed Owen with my head bowed. There were rocks in my stomach. A short stone path led from the boardwalk down a tiny hill around the big red building. A great big wooden gate was flung open to reveal the huge patio alight with a happiness I couldn't feel.

The patio was outlined with a single string of fairy lights strung up by poles at each corner. The little lights threw an almost magical glow over the patio where a few people danced and even more stood around talking. Several men with guitars sat in a jumble in the corner, alternately talking and playing. There was a long, low table off to the right, littered with drinks and punch bowls.

"Bingo," Benjamin slurred. The bimbo was at his heels.

Immediately to the left of the gate, Mr. Hall sat in a metal folding chair, tapping his foot rhythmically but seemingly out of tempo with the acoustic guitar. More rocks tumbled down my throat and settled in my stomach with a crash. My two worlds were colliding, and I wasn't prepared for it.

In my haste to not find Rory, I let my guard down. Somebody else found me.

"What are you doing here?"

Jen Johnson stood before me like an angel in a flowery, nearly sheer white dress. Her long blonde hair flowed in easy waves over her shoulders. Perfect beach waves Rosie spent hours trying to get. Jen looked as though she'd been born that way. I stood like a caricature of a teenage girl in front of her.

"Hi," I said lamely.

She rolled her eyes. "Are you here to see Rory?" she demanded.

I stuttered but managed to shake my head. "Just here with some friends." I began to gesture behind me, but quickly dropped my hand. They'd all scurried off, except Owen.

She shot a glaring look over my shoulder at Owen and then slipped silently away across the dance floor. Couples were beginning to emerge there, twirling with greater energy.

"What a bitch," Owen muttered. He weaved his arm around my waist to lead me toward the drinks table. I slipped out of his grasp and twirled around.

"Ten minutes tops," I said.

"What? Why?"

"No, you know what, I want to leave *now*." I stamped my foot like a petulant toddler.

"Let's just—"

"Cora?"

No, no, no, no. I twirled back around too quickly to compose my face.

No!

"Come to celebrate Lúnasa?" he said loudly over the music from some distance away.

Shit.

Though my face must have looked like a deer at the point of impact with a Range Rover, Rory was smiling from ear to ear. His smile absolutely lit up his face. He waltzed through the crowd with complete ease, but when he came to a standstill in front of me, I got the distinct impression that his eyes were nervous.

"Rory?" I said weakly. "What are you doing here?" In my haste to compose my voice, my content faltered.

He laughed it off. "I was about to ask the same of you." But he didn't wait for an actual explanation. "Do you need a drink?" He gestured toward my empty hands.

I shrugged lamely. Words were obviously failing me today.

He moved purposefully off toward the punch bowl, and I followed awkwardly. *God*, he looked good. He wore a blue t-shirt that fit just well enough to remind me that it had been a long, long time since I'd seen him with his shirt off. He wore khaki shorts and a worn pair of tennis shoes without laces. He turned and handed me a cup full of red juice.

Dear God, I hope this is spiked.

"It's Owen, right?"

I realized with a jolt that Owen was, indeed, still with us. His existence had quite slipped my mind.

"We met a while back," Rory said, extending his hand.

Owen, however, was not interested in small talk. He didn't actually acknowledge that Rory had spoken, and instead shuffled away with a mumbled declaration of a need to find beer.

"Are you having—I mean, I know you don't know anyone—

but—"

"I just got here," I heard myself say, "but I'm having a blast."

Neither of us spoke for a moment. *Why is he making me so nervous?* Why wasn't he talking? Maybe it was the fact that I had just crashed the first—and last—party of my crashing career, and it just so happened to be his. I steered carefully clear of that thought, which would only make my hands shake worse.

"Is Mrs. O'Leary here?" I asked.

"No, no, she doesn't leave her house much."

Once again, we plunged into silence. Why these nerves? Screw the party, it was definitely that shirt. Or those arms! *Stop looking at his arms!*

"And how did you—I mean—" He laughed uneasily. "We've just never had anyone from the big houses here."

"Yeah, I—my friends—" I could hear Benjamin guffawing loudly at something Owen was saying. I definitely didn't want to associate with them now. "This is awkward," I finished weakly.

He laughed. "It doesn't need to be," he said. "You know half the people here already. I can give you the lowdown on anybody you don't know." He came up to stand next to me so we could face the others and point. I played along and let him explain the most infamous of the locals.

He pointed out his mother, his father, a few people I would never remember, a few Johnson children, and I added my own commentary to them all. Spiked or not, the punch was doing its job; I was talking more than I intended.

"All these people celebrate Loo—uh …?" I trailed off.

He laughed. "Lúnasa." He pronounced it *LOO-nah-suh*. "And no, as far as I know, nobody in Oyster Beach knows what Lúnasa is. Or anyone in Ireland, for that matter. It's a really ancient Celtic holiday. It's more of a way for my parents to remind people they're Irish."

I glanced toward where Mrs. O'Brien was unloading more food from a trolley onto the long table near the back of the office building. Aidan stood nearby, helping. "So what *is* Lúnasa?"

"It was a harvest festival. It marked the beginning of the harvest season. They celebrated the god Lugh and all the food the Earth gave them. It was apparently a really crazy party. Poetry, music, games, dancing—all the modern makings of a party, at least. They also had this weird tradition called … damn, what were they called? I don't remember, but they were these trial marriages. Kind of like a blind marriage, a guy and a girl would hold hands through a wooden door, and they'd be married that way. But the marriage only lasted a year and a day, then they could both walk away from it. Like a trial run." He seemed to become embarrassed all of a sudden.

"With today's divorce rate, that could probably help America a bit," I said.

He grinned. "Sorry, I was rambling."

A loud booming laugh broke through our little world on the side of the patio.

"That really loud guy is Captain Harville," Rory said, as if to change the subject. "He's the head of the local police." The cop was boisterous and friendly, and when he noticed Rory pointing toward him, he bounded over.

"Miss Manchester! How are you doing?"

"I'm good, officer; thanks," I said.

Rory looked at me, perplexed.

"How nice of you to join us!" Captain Harville exclaimed. He carried a plastic cup filled with a golden-brown liquid. It smelled like something my dad kept in a cupboard at home. Perhaps whiskey. "You have to meet *everyone*! And, Cora—" Captain Harville's voice dropped a few decibels, as if in concern for the topic at hand. "You do remember Mr. Hall, don't you?"

I nodded weakly. A glance told me the old man was still perched on his folding chair in the corner. The sight of him flooded me with pity for Jen Johnson (which was the last thing I wanted to feel right now) and concern for Mrs. O'Leary.

"I'll just go wave him over—"

"Oh!" I exclaimed. "Please don't, he looks so comfortable …"

"I was actually just going to show Cora around a bit," Rory jumped in deftly. I eyed him with adoration. Could it possibly be that he wanted me to himself?

"Oh, all right then." The big cop's face fell. "I only mention it because he was asking about you only the other day."

My cheeks burned. Why on Earth would Mr. Hall do that?

Captain Harville took a sip of his drink, which seemed to reinvigorate him. He became bouncy again and finally left us after eliciting promises of everyone dancing later in the evening.

"How do you know Mr. Hall?" Rory asked when he'd gone. "Or Captain Harville, for that matter?"

"Mr. Hall was the one who … the one to … well, he was the one to help me when I found—I mean—"

But Rory was nodding in understanding. His eyes flicked involuntarily to the corner where Jen Johnson stood amid a gaggle of girls. Did I imagine her eyes were smoldering?

"He also …" I faltered. "He told me a lot about—"

And that's the unfortunate moment Mrs. O'Brien approached us to say hello. I was polite, and I was overly friendly, but even when she had wandered away, the chance was gone. It didn't feel right to talk about Mrs. O'Leary here, among everyone having a wonderful time without her.

Behind me, I heard snorts of derision from Blondie, in response to who knows what. It felt unnatural and out of place, her being here.

"You'll all be going home soon," Rory said absently.

"That will hardly be a tragedy for you."

Rory grinned. I loved the way he grinned. The corners of his mouth drew up sharply and his lips grew tight, revealing just the barest hint of white teeth beneath. "I think I'll miss some people," he said.

I heard Blondie call my name from somewhere behind me, but I blocked it out.

"Oh?" I said breathlessly.

Rory nodded and was silent a beat before saying, "Can I ask you a question?"

"Yeah?" I was already dreading it. He had a knack for embarrassing me.

"That night at the jetty, why were you crying? I mean, you were crying before Princess ever fell in the water."

I stared at the floor, willing myself to disappear and miraculously reappear somewhere far, far away. Like St. Louis. Or China. Perhaps Jupiter.

"And, I mean, I know I've thrown around my fair share of insults," he went on, "but they never fazed you. And, I do consider myself rather clever. So if my wit couldn't unsettle you, make you cry—not that I was trying! Anyway, I just … well, I just didn't know what on earth could get to you like that."

His insults never fazed me? If he only knew! I wanted to come up with a really good lie about the tears, but none of them seemed good enough for Rory.

"If you don't want to tell me," he finally said, "it's seriously okay."

"No, it's fine," I said. "I was just having a fight with someone." My eyes involuntarily flitted in the direction of Owen, where he was talking to a group of local girls. To my dismay, Rory followed this.

"Oh," he said, nodding his head slowly in a Mrs. O'Leary fashion. I watched as Blondie and the bimbo and Benjamin gathered around Owen, looking bored. "So he's your boyfriend?"

"What? I … no. No, no, he's not." I knew I was blushing, but perhaps it was too dark for him to notice. I waited a beat. "Is Jen …?"

"No," Rory said. "She's a good friend. The sister type."

I nodded. What was the appropriate follow-up to such a brazen question as that?

"It looks like that means we're both free to dance," Rory said. "That is, if you dance?" My stomach took flight. A slow song had just come on. That was certainly something I could muster up some dancing skills for—at least some mediocre swaying. But Owen suddenly moved in my peripheral vision. He had removed himself from the local girls, and the others were looking around for me.

"Um …"

"Cora!" Blondie was gesturing for me to join her as the others headed for the exit. She looked incredulous that I was taking this long to disengage myself from a local boy. Owen saw her gesturing and his eyes zeroed in on what he could only assume was an unnecessarily long conversation with Rory.

"You're welcome to stay," Rory said softly, almost inaudibly.

The little lights were making everything glow in a strangely surreal way. There were lightning bugs dotting the darkness beyond the party, giving the night a soft friendly glow.

But in looking at Owen across the patio, I could hear echoes of my mother's angry voice.

But *Jesus!* Rory's eyes were gorgeous. *So big, so brown. So very, very big and brown.*

"I don't think I can." I spoke just as quietly as he had.

I turned quickly away, avoiding his magical eyes. I just barely saw him nodding slowly, but I couldn't bring myself to look back as I joined the others, loitering near the gate. A few were already pushing down the walkway toward the boardwalk. They were loud and unapologetic.

"God that was so boring," Blondie said.

"Did you see that girl with the pink dress?" the bimbo shrieked. "It looked like a Barbie dress. Seriously, I had one just like it for my

Barbies."

Aidan O'Brien stood leaning against the fence with two other boys I didn't recognize. I caught him looking at me as we walked past. I walked as quickly as possible out of his sight.

When we reached the boardwalk, I felt it was safe to glance back. Aidan and friends were joining the party again. Rory was standing right where I'd left him, on the edge of the patio, gazing absently into the throng of dancing couples. He had the tiniest trace of a lost smile on his lips, and his hands were resting in his pockets. But the effect was quite different from Owen's signature stance. Owen always looked like he was posing. Rory looked, well, dejected. And for some twisted reason, this made my stomach do a few happy somersaults.

Coilíneacht
A COLONY

OUTSIDE ON THE BOARDWALK, IT BECAME apparent that Benjamin Huston was harboring a great number of beers under his polo shirt. It became apparent because he tripped and they all came spilling out onto the boardwalk with a series of unbroken thuds. He tried to hand the bottles out to the group, but the ones on the ground were already rolling away.

"Shh!" the bimbo spluttered drunkenly.

"You stole their beer?" Owen said. He'd taken the words right out of my mouth. But there was a smile on his face.

"That was really rude," I said.

Benjamin hadn't even heard me, but the bimbo was incredulous that I would dare to insult her hero.

"That was rude of *you* to say that," she shot back.

"I just don't think you need to steal from people

who ..." I trailed off. *Who had less than us.*

The unspoken words twisted in my throat. Did I really regard the people back there as a charity case? Rory and his family and his friends and neighbors?

"Who *what?*" the bimbo demanded, daring me to finish that complicated sentence. When I didn't answer she stalked off ahead of me.

We were passing Mrs. O'Leary's house, and I slowed unconsciously. The little yellow house was dark. What was she doing in there by herself while the rest of the town was at a party? *She's nearly always alone. What does she do?*

"Hey, forget about it all," Owen said, breaking into my consciousness. I was obviously trying very hard to do just that. I looked at him blankly. "They're nice people, and you have a huge heart."

I didn't say anything.

"Let's go have some fun," he said.

The rest of the group had stopped to wait for us a little ahead, but they were all tangled in their own conversations. Only the bimbo still glared at me between watching Benjamin stumble around as he tried to stand still.

"Hey—Cora." Owen turned my chin to face him. I was disappointed that he could read my thoughts so clearly. "Forget about them. All of them." He waved vaguely toward the others. "They're drunk and annoying, I know. Let's go back to my place, just you and me."

I didn't resist as he steered me after the others. "My parents are gone for the weekend," he went on. My back stiffened. "You can spend the night, just you and me, and I'll walk you home in the morning." I stopped walking.

Was that why he'd been hanging around me all summer? He wanted to sleep with me? Little did he know I was a virgin, one with little experience in any of the romantic arts. And—

"Oh *my* God!" Benjamin yelled. To my utter horror, he had been listening. He rolled his eyes dramatically. "Will you sleep with the guy already? We've been listening to him *whining* about it all freaking summer! We're so *sick* of it!"

A cold crept over my heart as I realized all the thoughts and evenings and laughs I'd wasted on Owen Carlton that summer. *A nice guy* was the conclusion I had drawn. *Different from the others.* When in fact, he had been going around babbling to his friends about how I wouldn't sleep with him. We weren't even in a relationship!

Everything in my body froze. I was waiting for Owen to protest, to debunk it as a drunken lie. Or even to half-heartedly tell Benjamin to shut up. Even that would have been enough. But he didn't.

Instead, he laughed.

I tore away from Owen and stalked away from the group. There was only one way to avoid them: I headed south, toward my refuge.

"Cora—Cora, hey—come on, Cora!" Owen called after me.

Benjamin's voice was the last thing I heard. "Oh, let her go, she's such a freaking tease."

At the pier, I sat down right at the edge where it sloped into the water. The surface of the water was rather still in the hot night, but it still lapped gently over the edge and onto my bare legs. The waves were unnaturally warm.

I didn't want to cry, I had been crying so damn much lately. Which was *not* how it was supposed to be. Rosie had always regarded me as some kind of stonehearted fortress. She was always crying over boys, and I never was. Well this summer would have provided a nice role reversal. I didn't really think I would cry this time—I wasn't sad, I was angry. *Angry as hell.* But that just brought angry tears to my eyes. It wasn't long before I was huffing and heaving, expending most of my energy trying to fight back the tears. For some reason my sorrow always brought me back to Mrs. O'Leary. Visions of dead bodies and seals and ashrays danced before my eyes, mingling with the tears. Selkies and more dead bodies and Jen Johnson.

"Hey, do you have a death wish?"

I nearly toppled off the edge of the pier in fright.

"As I recall, you can't swim."

I looked over my shoulder, eyes puffy and nose dripping despite my best efforts. "How do you *do* that?" I demanded. "Whenever I turn into a crumpling mess, whenever I shed a tear—there you are! It's like you always catch me at my worst!"

He didn't answer. He came and sat down next to me. The smile was gone from his face. "I didn't know you were crying this time," he said.

I wiped my eyes and sniffed loudly. "I'm not crying."

His face cracked into that grin of his. He tried to stifle it. "It's okay; I get caught not crying all the time."

There was a marked difference in him. He was so much calmer here on the pier.

"How did you know?" I said. "That night when Princess fell in, I mean. How did you know I was crying? You appeared out of nowhere."

"You're on *my* jetty, you know," he said. "Such a little princess. Goes wherever she wants. I guess it's my fault for not marking it properly. I'll have to invest in some signs." *His* jetty. No wonder he was so calm here.

I snorted and he nudged me with his elbow. I rocked sideways into the water and righted myself. My toes were warm in the water.

"Are we done not crying? It gets tiring."

"I think we're done," I said, sniffing loudly.

We sat in silence as my mind wandered to every corner of my being, searching for something interesting to say. Rory was comfortable in the silence, but my body was bursting with too many emotions to be silent. I finally asked, "What's spring tide?"

Rory chortled a bit. "Uh, I think it's around the full moon and the new moon, when the tide gets the highest and lowest. That's when it has the longest range. Why? Is that what you were crying about?"

"Not crying," I clarified once again. "I was just thinking of Mrs. O'Leary. She told me once that that's the only time the selkies can change." I paused, wondering if he thought about Mrs. O'Leary's fairytales as much as I did. Or at all. For some reason, I knew that I would be disappointed if I learned that he didn't. "Do you think Seamus's soul is down there? In a merman's cage?"

"Jesus, you do need cheering up." He laughed gruffly.

"Have any of the other sailors been found? Mr. Hall said there were two left."

Rory sighed. "Todd Phillips was. Washed up on shore."

I was silent. Another body on land, another soul in the cage, lodged in the sand of the ocean bottom. Was there a woman somewhere who was still madly in love with Todd Phillips?

"Hey, you're really depressing me. Do you want to see something that might cheer you up?" Rory said. "I mean, it's pretty warm tonight, it should be good."

I wiped my eyes and rubbed my cheeks. The tears had run dry, though my face was still wet. And I could tell he wanted desperately to avoid more of my tears. "Sure," I half-said, half-sniffed.

He jumped up and grabbed my still-wet hand. Even through my haze of tears and confused sadness, something magical shot through my arm like electricity. This wasn't like when Owen held my hand. This … this was *magical.* I got up and let him pull me down the pier and farther south, away from the big houses and away from town. He was nearly running.

"Where are we going?" I asked.

He stopped abruptly and spun around. "Two things," he said. He held up one finger, "Do not talk." He held up another finger, "Do not make a sound."

I smirked. "That's kind of the same thing."

"Just promise," he demanded.

"Okay."

"That's not good enough."

"I promise?" I said.

He raised his eyebrows.

"I pinky promise?" I tried again.

He extended a pinky, and I linked mine around his. "There is nothing in this world more binding than a pinky promise."

He whirled off again, his hand firmly holding mine. We stumbled awkwardly, half-running, for just a few more minutes. The beach was rocky here, but we came to a great sand dune perched on a small piece of land that jutted out into the ocean. Here, he stopped and began to carefully climb the dune. He pressed a finger to his lips as a reminder and moved stealthily.

Near the middle of the dune, he got down on his hands and knees and crawled to the top. There, he lay flat on his belly and peeked over.

I stood at the bottom, watching him. When he realized I wasn't following, he looked at me with a grin that made my knees weak and gestured for me to follow, nodding over the crest of the dune.

I scrambled up after him. Near the top, I crouched down next to him and peeked over. A gasp escaped involuntarily, and despite his rules, Rory grinned.

Below stretched a long wall of the dune that swept toward the sea and ended in a rocky jumble near the water. But below us, amid a group of smooth rocks at the meeting of the dune and the coast, was a small knot of sleeping seals. They were all bunched up, almost like they were cuddling. There were little clusters of them, snuggling. One was even laying on top of two others. They were still and silent, and I felt like we were intruding on something sacred.

Rory nodded toward the water. There in the dark, on a wet rock that jutted out into the waves, was a lone seal. He wasn't sleeping, and his eyes, looking in our direction, glowed in the night. The moon reflected a deep golden color in them. He must not have seen us, for he didn't react. I waited for him to bark—or make whatever noise seals make—and wake the others. But he didn't. Eventually he turned back to the water.

I was watching the seals, but I was very conscious of how close I was to Rory. His left arm was curled around my back, so that his mouth was perfectly even with my ear. I felt warm and protected against him, with the wind whipping ruthlessly around us. It couldn't touch me.

When he breathed, it tickled my ear.

"How many do you think are selkies?" He had said it so quietly, so close to my ear, it was more like breathing. Like we didn't need to talk to communicate.

I couldn't answer, considering I'd been sworn to silence, but when I craned my neck around, Rory was watching me, not the seals.

For a brief millisecond, I thought we were going to kiss. But then he swallowed and looked back out at the peaceful scene in front of us. I let myself relax into the sand beneath his arm, protected from the wind and the swirling sand, and watched the seals sleep.

Suddenly, Rory plucked something from the sand right beside me. One of the tin whistles had fallen out of my pocket. His face was lit with excitement. "Where did you get this?" he mouthed.

I put my finger to my lips, mocking his rules. He shook his head and twirled the whistle deftly around his fingers like he was performing a practiced trick.

I would never have tired of that, lying there pressed into his side, watching the seals sleep. But he eventually motioned for us to go. He turned away and climbed down the dune without looking back, no parting glance for the seals, as if he did this all the time. I, however, kept looking over my shoulder for one last peaceful glance until they were out of sight.

When we were far enough not to disturb the animals, Rory turned to me, wielding the whistle. "You little thief!" His face was bright with a smile. "Where did you find this?"

"On the jetty," I said. "Is it yours?"

He didn't answer, but banged the whistle on his palm, holes facing down. Then he picked at the holes with a fingernail and banged it some more. When we were back in familiar territory, he seemed to be satisfied. He stopped and blew into the whistle, hard and sure. Sand puffed out, and he dashed to the water and dunked it in the waves. He put it to his lips again and embarked upon a litany of clear, high-pitched notes. It was, somehow, exactly how I'd expected it to sound, when played correctly, but at the same time completely foreign.

He raised his eyebrows as he played, as if to ask my approval. Approval was an understatement. The music seeped through my skin, went right to my veins. My courage was lifted past any previous level in my life by the little ditty that mixed and broke away from the sounds of the ocean and distant sounds of revelry. It was as if what I was about to do next was preordained.

I grabbed the whistle from his mouth a little too roughly. Playfully, he held on, but then I kissed him and both our hands fell gently to our sides. I just leaned over and kissed him! Rosie would *never* believe it.

His lips were soft and both of our lips tasted fleetingly of salt. He kissed gently, as if to heal every time he'd ever caught me with tears in my eyes. His left hand skimmed my arm and landed next to my neck, just the tips of his fingers resting against my throat. My whole body warmed under that touch, slight though it was.

The reality of what I'd just done hit me quickly, and my stomach flipped. I'd just kissed a boy. *Without knowing whether he wanted to kiss me.* I pulled away abruptly, no longer sure of what to do with my lips. Or my limbs, for that matter. But apparently neither did he. We were both still holding the tin whistle.

I hazarded a glance up at Rory's face in time to see a grin slowly forming there.

"If you didn't like my music, all you had to do was say so."

An Athair
THE FATHER

I THOUGHT ABOUT THE SCENE AS I FELL ASLEEP AT night and even called Rosie to share the news, censoring facts about who he was and how angry my parents would be. I replayed the scene over and over in my head, going over how I could have done it differently. How I should have told him all about everything Mr. Hall had told me. How I didn't have to scuttle home immediately after kissing him, embarrassment flooding my cheeks. But that's what I had done.

He had called after me once. "Hey, your whistle!"

"It's not yours?" I asked, still backing away.

He shook his head.

"What about this?" I plucked the silver one from my other pocket and held it up.

He was nothing short of shocked. "A regular little thief." His grin was crooked. I was just short of swooning.

I ran back to him to show him the silver whistle. "Where did you get this one?" he asked.

"The yard of the fabulous Ritz estate," I said in my best British accent. "I'm gonna give it back to Mrs. O'Leary."

I didn't see his face as I turned, my dress whirling satisfactorily, and pranced home, utterly on top of the world.

But now, as I made my way past Mrs. O'Leary's every day, I regretted not having stayed. Not having made plans, gotten his phone number, made a tin can telephone, *anything!* I was too chicken to go directly to the resort and ask for him, but I walked hopefully by the little yellow house every day … okay, several times a day. But he was never there. And, more surprisingly, neither was Mrs. O'Leary.

I was sure she was inside, but I felt some unspoken agreement that what we had was restricted to the porch. I felt it would be intruding to call on her in her little house, where she retreated each evening. She had always retreated reluctantly, but with an air of relief too, as if it was only in the little house that she could get away from the constant nagging of the ocean.

Mr. Hall came back to the Pink Palace for what my mother termed a "follow-up" visit, as if the house was ill and in desperate need of a doctor. Which is, more or less, how my mother viewed it. This time, despite the unpleasant memories and thoughts he brought up, I didn't shy away from the man. It was as if my night with Rory had given me the courage to face the things about Mrs. O'Leary that I hadn't wanted to face before.

As soon as my mother left the kitchen, I stopped rummaging through the refrigerator and turned to the older man. "What happened to the babies?"

He looked unsettled, but not altogether surprised.

I walked quickly to the table and sat down across from him. "The O'Leary babies," I pressed on. "What happened to them?"

"I don't know," he said. "I already told you all that I know."

I didn't believe that for a second. "Well, who was with them when they disappeared? You don't leave a newborn on its own."

Mr. Hall looked at me evenly. "Lia was with them both."

I could read the accusation in his voice. But I didn't believe it. She couldn't have—not intentionally …

"Well what does she say happened? Did she say somebody else—"

"Do you really think you're the first person to wonder? People have been wondering that for fifty years."

"And? What have they come up with?"

"Well, the prevailing idea among the townspeople at the time was that the boys drowned. The both of them. And that she facilitated it."

My mouth fell open. "That's ridiculous," I said simply.

Mr. Hall shrugged. "So is the disappearance of two children under the same mother's care within years of one another. It's not as though her life was perfect. Their marriage … well, there were problems. You might not want to believe that, but there were. Oh, there were problems."

I let the thought drift into the silence, hoping it would evaporate there. But Mr. Hall interrupted it.

"You know the two youngest O'Brien boys very well, don't you?"

Oh Jesus. Was I about to be lectured by this old man on who I spent my time with? He had to have been speaking to my mother about it!

"I know them," I said cryptically.

"Then you know that they were adopted?"

"Yes," I said defensively. Though, in all honesty, I hadn't considered that Aidan was adopted, as well. *Of course.* He was the spitting image of Rory. "Why is this relevant?"

"Seamus arranged it all," Mr. Hall explained. "He knew the girl that gave birth to both of the boys. She couldn't raise them herself. First the older lad. She couldn't take care of him, and the O'Briens adopted him. Then it happened again, and the O'Briens took the younger one, too. Poor, unfortunate girl or naïve, dumb girl, nobody could agree. It was a time of great scandal for the city."

"I still don't see how this is relevant," I said, getting a bit annoyed.

"Do you know, people talked, as people do, and many came up with some very outlandish conjectures. People wondered why Seamus cared so much, about this baby born of some unknown girl. When it happened a second time, during a period when times were even harder with his marriage, well, many people said that it must be—it *had* to be—his child. Why else would he care so much?"

I laughed outright. Rather loudly. "Are you trying to say that people thought Mr. O'Leary cheated on his wife and fathered Rory and Aidan with some girl?"

"It's not as crazy a tale as you're making it sound. It was quite strange, Seamus caring so much about an unknown girl's illegitimate children. And his own marriage so full of tragedy. Not having any of his own children to raise. And Lia being so depressed in those days. It was considered a natural progression that he should find love elsewhere."

"*Natural?*" I demanded with disgust.

"Well. One can at least see how it was thought that perhaps Seamus was the father of those boys."

But, but Mr. O'Leary would have been … *old* when Rory and Aidan were born. Though of course I knew it was still *possible*, biologically speaking. And I wasn't about to bring up the topic of aging sexuality with Mr. Hall. So instead, I asked, "If Seamus was their father, then why would he not raise them himself?"

Mr. Hall was silent.

"If they were his own kids, why would he just dish them out to the most willing neighbor and never say anything about it?"

Again, the man was silent.

I realized with a jolt that I was actually buying the logic of this theory. A cold began crawling up my back. Was the boy who was helping Mrs. O'Leary every day actually the son of her unfaithful husband's lover? Was the husband Mrs. O'Leary still yearned for, still waited for, actually a cheating jerk?

"You were his best friend!" I shouted. "Don't you know whether it's true or not?"

"Friendship has its limits."

I couldn't tell if he was talking about his friendship with Seamus or the beating I was giving our flimsy acquaintance. But I was nowhere near done.

"What happened to Seamus?" I asked.

"He disappeared."

"I know that."

Mr. Hall looked at me sharply. I stared right back. The way he had of implying things about Mrs. O'Leary, things I didn't like, made me courageous. I could stand up against this man. For her.

"He was alone," Mr. Hall finally said. "He used to go out to fish alone. One day he never came back."

I remembered what Rory had said once, about what the townspeople thought. "Was it suicide?"

Mr. Hall appraised my face, apparently impressed that I'd done my homework. "I don't think so."

"Did they find his body?"

"It's not every day that fishing accidents yield tangible evidence." He paused. "You experienced an exception to that rule."

My face reddened. A giant merman reared up in my mind, swinging a giant, iron cage around his head. The cage held the souls of Jen Johnson's brother and Seamus O'Leary, and now Mrs. O'Leary was in there, too. Nothing made sense to me anymore.

I rubbed my throbbing head and raked through my confused thoughts for another question to settle this mess. But my mother returned then.

"I think we need more mirrors," she announced, oblivious to the sea of emotions in the room.

I excused myself as politely as I could muster and ran upstairs, as if the faster I ran, the farther I could get from the heartache I was feeling for a young Lia O'Leary.

Stoirm Mhór
A GREAT STORM

THOUGH IT FELT LIKE AGES, IN REALITY IT WAS only a few days after the party at the resort that I ran into Owen again. I had started the morning at Mrs. O'Leary's and, unable to find her or Rory, I began to wander back down the beach. I had been left with too much to think about by my conversation with Mr. Hall. All along I'd thought Mrs. O'Leary was the crazy one—but was it possible that Mr. Hall was actually the one losing his marbles? Could Rory actually be the son of Mr. O'Leary? And moreover, could Mrs. O'Leary *know*? Surely Rory didn't know. I just knew in my heart that he would have told me had he known. It felt wrong for me, an outsider, to be holding all this knowledge—or conjecture—that Rory didn't seem to know. I carried the blue pail, full of shells, but my mind was a million miles away in an Oyster Beach that existed decades ago.

"You coming out with us tonight?"

I was startled out of my reverie and looked up to find Owen standing a few feet away, having just come down from the boardwalk.

After collecting my wits, I shook my head.

"So you're still angry?"

The bimbo and the Huston kid stood awkwardly behind Owen up on the boardwalk, and some boys I didn't know waited impatiently behind them.

"Cora, come on, there's only a handful of days left," Owen said. "There's no point spending them being angry."

"I think I'll spend them doing what I like, thank you," I said curtly.

He rolled his eyes. "We both know you're going to get over it in like two days."

My mouth was open to protest, but Benjamin did it for me.

"Jesus, Owen, why do you care? If she's going to be frigid, forget about her."

I was seething but too full of potent anger to form any real words.

"Dude, come on!" one of the strange boys on the boardwalk called. Benjamin grinned at me and moved off after the other boys. Owen watched him go.

"Whatever," he finally said. "Let me know when you get over it." And he stalked off after them.

The bimbo stood awkwardly, drifting off toward the boys, but her eyes were on me and they looked sympathetic. I wanted to shout something mean to her, to make her run off after them and stop staring at me, but my brain was still addled with anger.

To my utter astonishment she stopped. And then with one look thrown over her shoulder, she came toward me. "I don't know if it means anything to you, but I think they're assholes," she said.

I was stunned. "Thanks?" I said, unsure of the sincerity of the claim.

"Especially Benjamin," she said quietly. That was certainly a heavy accusation coming from his formerly simpering number-one fan.

"I thought you liked him," I said lamely.

She shrugged. "I guess I didn't really know he was a jerk." It was an answer too simple for my taste, but for the present moment it would have to do. Neither of us were exactly great conversationalists.

"Well thanks for letting me know," I said.

"And Owen's not too bad," she added.

I snorted. The last thing I wanted was a defense of Owen Carlton.

"I mean it," she said. "He just gets caught up with those guys, and, I don't know, everybody gets caught up in it sometimes."

I don't, I wanted to say, but I bit my tongue.

"I think he means well."

"We can agree to disagree," I said diplomatically.

"I think you're cooler than any of them." She said it as though it was the highest of compliments. I knew it was intended to be.

"Thanks," I mumbled. I didn't mention that I didn't care what my "cool" factor was anymore.

There was an awkward silence. She finally asked what I was doing, indicating the blue bucket.

"Collecting shells," I replied.

"Can I help?"

"Don't you have to catch up with them?" I nodded toward the group in the distance that seemed to be making its way toward Main Street.

She watched them for a second and then shook her head. "I think I might qualify as frigid, too." Her face broke into a smile, and I couldn't help but return it.

That afternoon I learned more about her than I had all summer. She asked a lot of questions about my family, and so I asked a lot about hers. I felt uncomfortable at first, divulging my stories to someone so obviously at the inner ring of that world I was completely consumed with hating at the present moment. But before long I had forgotten that she lived north of the Pink Palace and when we parted on the boardwalk at dinnertime, I was in a legitimately good mood.

I looked over my shoulder and watched her pad softly down the boardwalk, flip-flops in her hand.

"Louisa?" I called. She turned around. "Thanks," I said.

She smiled and waved and continued on her way.

When I went inside, my parents were in the kitchen, which was odd in itself. My mom preferred to eat in the dining room, and Dad didn't normally stand around chatting while she fixed dinner. But they seemed to have been in the middle of a pressing conversation when I walked in.

Mom was dicing tomatoes rather sloppily, and Princess sat at her feet waiting for a misguided chunk to hit the floor.

Dad looked up from the dining room doorway when I walked in. He pulled his hands from his pockets and crossed them over his chest.

"Cora, will you sit down a minute?"

My blood immediately grew hot, indignant already at whatever outrageous conversation was about to befall me. But I sat obediently. The kitchen table was cold and clean, rarely used. The chair was chilly and unfamiliar, and the ceiling fan whirred softly, methodically. Except for a cursory glance at my entrance, Mom's eyes were trained on the tomatoes.

"What's for dinner?" I tried.

"Cora, we need to talk about this year," Dad said. "We've been letting it go, but it's gone on long enough. The simple fact is that I'm not telling my acquaintances that my lovely daughter is a college dropout. George Arnold—"

"Well, you won't have to, because one has to start college to drop out."

"Cora, you're acting like an idiot."

Mom stopped chopping but remained silent. Dad remained perfectly still in the doorway, not moving, nothing but his jaw and the angry vein in his neck working furiously.

"I talked to George Arnold today—"

"Dad, I'm not—"

"What *exactly* do you envision yourself doing this year?" he shouted. Princess watched him, ears alert, head cocked in confusion. He normally deferred rule of the house to my mother. Yelling was reserved for very serious occasions. I had learned to avoid these as I was growing up. But at the present moment, I was glad he was yelling. I wanted him to yell so that I could yell right back.

"You know what I want to do!" I said shrilly. "I want to travel, I want to see the world! We have the money to do it, what is *wrong* with you? Other people would die for the chance, *die* for the chance to travel like I could! We have the money, *you* have the money! I would work; I would pay you back! You have the means to give me that chance and you won't! You should be thankful we have that chance!"

"You're talking like a spoiled brat," Dad said.

"I *am* a spoiled brat!" I shrieked. It had never sounded so true. "You've given me everything, except what I actually want! You don't even understand what I want—you never have. I want to take a year off because I don't know what in the hell I want to do with my life! I don't want to major in something as ridiculous and boring as *business management* so that I can hate my life for the remainder of my years after graduation!"

It was out in the open now.

"It's a major, Cora, it doesn't determine the rest of your life," Mom said softly.

"Oh, you're *exactly* the person I want to be hearing advice from!" I yelled. It was mean and it was low, but I was feeling too strong to stop myself. "*Please*, let me follow in your footsteps! I so need to learn the art of finding someone eager enough to run a *shoe company* that he will *condescend* to marry me!" Neither of them stopped me. I don't know why neither of them stopped me. "That way, I won't have to stick to my

B.S. in business management, which I never intended to actually use, and I can spend the rest of my days organizing parties for old women who have seen so little of the world that they're content to sit and talk about their husbands and their children and businesses they know nothing about so long as they're plastered by four p.m.!"

They could have interrupted. Thrown a shoe at my head. Sprayed me in the face with water. But nobody stopped me.

"Why are we even *here?* What was the logic there? That if we go to the beach and everybody enjoys it, then we'll forget all about this weird, *insane,* crippling fear of water that has gripped this psycho family for, like, twenty years? Yeah, that'll make us all forget she ever existed!"

The silence that followed felt like weights on my brain. Mom stood, arms hanging limply at her sides, knife still in one hand. Dad stared at me, eyes squinted, as if I had disappeared into thin air and he could find no trace of a person before him.

And finally, he broke the silence. "You're going to Western," he said evenly, calmly.

I gulped, the lie on my lips. I wasn't ready for that confession yet. For them to know that I irrevocably could *not* attend Western University. "I never got a letter—"

"You will," he said.

I scoffed.

"It's your dream school, I don't know why—"

"It's not my dream school," I said.

"It *was* your dream school—"

I was on my feet and screaming now. "It was not *my* dream to go to Western! It was *your* dream!"

I whipped around and left the room as quickly as possible. These were the most hurtful words I'd ever spoken to my parents. I didn't want to see the effect. I was too angry to let it be marred by anything like pity.

Compoird sa Stoirm
COMFORT IN THE STORM

THE PORCH DOOR SLAMMED BEHIND ME, BUT Princess had slipped out first. There was some doubt in my mind where I would end up, but not for Princess, who hadn't seen her good friend in a long time. She started running once she realized I intended to. She bounded ahead of me, her little feet pounding the boardwalk to Mrs. O'Leary's tiny yellow house.

With her recent track record of invisibility, I hadn't expected Mrs. O'Leary to be outside, but I wasn't prepared for the person who was. Rory looked up just in time to see me stop short in the front yard, panting, eyes streaming.

Jesus! Why was he *always* around when I was crying?

Princess had already jumped up the stairs and stood pressed against his legs, imploring him to scratch her back.

"Cora, what's wrong?"

I backed away abruptly. He got the hint.

"Where's Mrs. O'Leary?" I asked.

"She's inside," he said, lingering on the bottom step. "I think she's going to sleep."

The tears were fast and I knew I looked like a tomato, but I wasn't ready to let my guard down just yet. "Where were you?" I finally squeaked out. He was confused. It was clear on his face. "Where was Mrs. O'Leary?" I added. "She hasn't been out here recently."

"She's been sick," he said. He seemed to be weighing how much to tell me. I didn't blame him. My current state obviously hinted at some mental instability. "She's been pretty weak lately. The doctor's been in nearly every day."

My heart plummeted. *Selfish, selfish Cora.* Of course I hadn't even bothered to worry about her.

"Is she okay?"

He nodded. "She misses you. Talks about you to anyone who will listen." I sniffed loudly, and he took a tentative step off the stairs. "I missed seeing you around, too."

I was silent. *Act detached. Act detached.* That's what Rosie would have advised. *Don't let on that you think about that kiss all the time. Act detached. Detached!* But I was still crying. "I'm gonna go home," I mumbled, stumbling backward.

He stepped in front of me. "Cora, stop, you're obviously not okay."

"It's nothing you'd understand," I said.

I'd forgotten how warm his eyes were. Just looking at them made my insides melt. And the way the corner of his lip curled up in a pathetic smile hit me in the gut. "Try me?"

A sobbing, blubbering mess, I told him everything I'd said to my parents. We sat on the pier, legs dangling over the edge at first. But when it was clear I was beyond composure, Rory put his arm around me and I collapsed into a puddle in his arms, like a sun-caught ashray.

He sat, one arm around me, one around Princess, and before I knew it, I was telling him things that I had previously thought quite unrelated to my fight with my parents. I told him about Rosie and her never-ending line of boyfriends. To my later mortification, I found myself telling him about Josh Watson. I told him about the swimming lessons I tried to go to at the beginning of the summer and the swimming lessons I'd gone to when I was young. Oyster Beach seemed a thousand miles away as I told him all about the little girl who had drowned before I was born. And somehow, in some way completely unbeknownst to me, I concluded with,

"And I just want … I just want"—sniff—"I just want to live in Mrs. O'Leary's attic and"—sniff—"and I'd just talk about selkies with her for … for the rest of my life."

Rory laughed.

"Am-am I crazy?" I sputtered, wiping my eyes.

"It's quite possible," Rory said. I snorted a particularly unattractive sound.

The pier was lashing more violently than usual in the waves. I vaguely remembered something about a storm in the forecast, and I vividly remembered Mrs. O'Leary's account of the dog days.

"Regardless, you should go home now, it's got to be past midnight," he said.

"I'm not going home," I said.

"Why?"

"I've never said things like that to them before. I can't go home. Not yet. I'll wait here until they wake up and leave the house, go about their day, then I'll go home."

"Cora, they'll be worried sick."

I shook my head. "I'm more careful than even my mom after a few margaritas. They know that."

Rory looked as though he was about to protest, and I didn't expect him to understand, but at that exact moment, I distracted the both of us. I had an idea so wonderful, I did something more courageous than I had ever done before. I let go of his hand and ran off the pier. I came around to the side of the pier, right up to the gentle waves. I ripped off my shoes (and nothing else, not quite *that* courageous) and took a few tentative steps into the water.

"What in the hell are you doing?"

"I've got to learn sometime," I said. The water was past my knees now, but I was too scared to go farther. Rory was already behind me, standing at the cusp of the tide.

"Cora, it's dangerous," he said. "Come on."

It was stronger than I thought it would be. And I was more scared than I thought I would be. If seals were in this water, what the hell else could be in there?

"You don't understand the ocean; can you trust me? I swear I'll teach you, just not here with all the waves and undercurrents."

I didn't move.

"Let's go to the resort, I can get us into the pool there, just please will you get out of there?"

I suddenly began a retreat to the beach. "I have a better idea," I said and winked at him. I actually winked at him. A classic Caroline Manchester move. I was actually turning into my mother.

An Cúnamh Fostaigh
THE HIRED HELP

I CAN'T DO THIS, CORA," RORY SAID. HE STOOD beside the pool, throwing nervous glances up at the giant, sleeping house. Princess sat resignedly outside the white fence, watching us. I had never felt so brave in my life, and I was already sliding out of my shoes.

"What's the matter?" I said playfully. "Afraid the statues might be watching?" With a grin, I stepped cautiously down the steps into the shallow end of the pool. It was cold, but I resisted shivering and kept going until it was past my waist. God, I felt courageous.

But Rory's face was seriously worried, and he crossed his arms. He threw another anxious look up at the dark windows of the Ritz house. I'd thought sneaking in to use the massive Ritz pool was one of my better ideas. "I don't want to do this," Rory repeated.

Riding high on a million emotions raging inside me, I

stepped up to the side of the pool. I put on the most beguiling look I could muster and began to unbutton my dress. My fingers faltered on the second button. "And there's *nothing* I can do to change your mind?"

He groaned. I was relieved when he bent down and buttoned the one button I'd managed to undo. But my pride was a pinch wounded, too. "Well, if—"

"Cora, I could get fired."

I froze. "Please tell me you mean 'fired' as in set ablaze, and you're just really confused about science and—"

"Cora, I've been working here." He looked miserable as he stood back up.

"You *work* here? *Here?*"

He shrugged. "It started out with me just cleaning out Mr. O'Leary's shed and fixing some things, Mr. Hall got me the job, but then they had other stuff around and ..."

I didn't know why I was feeling fury inside, but I was. I stepped slowly out of the water and stood shivering and dripping by the stairs. "You work for the Ritzes?" I asked.

He nodded guiltily, like a toddler caught stealing cookies before dinner.

"Why didn't you tell me?"

He shrugged. "It never came up. Besides, things were going so well with you not hating me." His smile was easy. Why was he so goddamn easy-going and smiley? "I didn't think admitting to working for one of your friends would exactly be in my favor. I didn't know if you'd be mad at me or think less of me for it, but either way, I knew it wouldn't be good."

"They aren't my friends," I said coldly.

"Cora, why do you care?"

"Why do I care?" I repeated mutinously. "I care because I would rather spend time with you than worthless Marshall Ritz who has never worked a day in his life and probably never will. But the world's been intent on forcing me to hang out with him while you've been working away in his ridiculous house. With those *absurd* statues!"

I ran over and pounded my fist on a small cement woman dressed in the robes of ancient Athens. It only hurt my hand and I groaned in frustration.

Rory chuckled. It annoyed me. "Rory, I'm serious!"

He stifled a grin. That heart-stopping grin of his. "I know you are. But if I'm not mistaken, this you-wanting-to-hang-out-with-me thing is rather new."

Not as new as you think.

"But," he continued, "you've got time with me now."

I rolled my eyes. "I was talking—"

He reached me in two long strides and kissed me lightly on my lips, which were twitching in anger. It was enough to shut me up, which I think was the intention. Then he took my hand and pulled me back toward the boardwalk. "Come on, let's get out of here so that I get paid next week."

I let him lead me out of the yard, but walked slowly to keep some form of my petulance. At the back of the Pink Palace, he paused. Princess dashed away up the stairs and waited for me to open the screen door. The lights were still on inside, but the light in my parents' room was out. The house glowed softly in the night, framed by the darkness of the houses around it. The windows shone with a faint peachy rim, but the rest of it could have been black or green or any color at all in this light. It was almost pretty.

"Should I even bother telling you to go to bed?" Rory asked.

I shook my head. "I'm going to let Princess in, don't move," I said.

"You've got to at least change!" he hissed after me.

"That would be admitting defeat," I said.

We walked back along the boardwalk; I was barefoot but left large wet footprints on the wood.

"You *are* the most stubborn person I know."

"You have no idea," I said.

We kept walking, but near the resort, he paused again. "So I'm supposed to just leave you to sleep in a wet heap on the jetty?" he asked. "For the sharks or the morning swimmers to find you?"

"There are no sharks, and I'm not particularly afraid of the morning swimmers," I said.

He grinned. My heart beat furiously, but I wasn't up to the challenge of broaching the topic of my watching him swim yet. "I'm not going to sleep," I said quickly, to change the subject.

He groaned again, that half-annoyed, half-pleased sound from the depths of his stomach that I was beginning to enjoy. "Come on," he said. "I can get us into a cabin."

My stomach twisted and I stopped. "Rory—I'm not going to sleep with you," I blurted out.

He smiled, but kept walking. "That's okay; I've always thought sleeping was a solitary activity."

I ran a few paces. "You know what I mean! Rory, I'm serious!"

He stopped and turned to face me, this time his face serious. "I know. So am I. I would never make you do anything you don't want to do. It'll be warm in a cabin and we can sit down." I had never felt more comfortable taking his hand.

I did, however, feel vaguely guilty as he came out of the office with a ring of keys in hand and I followed him to cabin 24. But visions of a kind, cheery Mrs. O'Brien were the last thing my brain wanted at the moment, so I sat down at the kitchen table, my eyes on Rory.

There was a small block of wood in the middle of the table, with the same words painted across each side.

"What does that say?" I asked.

"*Céad míle fáilte*," he said. It sounded like "cad meel-ah fall-shuh."

I raised my eyebrows.

"It means, 'a hundred thousand welcomes.' It's Irish."

"I ..." ... *didn't know that was a language?*

"Most people here call it Gaelic, but over there, they just call it Irish. Not many people speak it anymore, but I'd like to learn." He disappeared into another room.

The fatigue hit me all at once. My eyes were heavy, and I moved to the couch across the combination kitchen-living room. I knew if I so much as put my head down, I'd be out like a light. I was also soaking wet, and so I perched on the edge of the couch instead.

"How did you know about the seals?" I asked. "The ones we went to see?"

"It's a resting colony, a haul-out. People aren't allowed to go down there, there's some sort of law, so everyone knows where they are."

"Are they always there?" I asked.

"No, around this time of year they go seek out secluded caves where they'll have their babies. Did you see their eyes? They have amazing eyes. They're huge and round and super complicated since they have to be able to focus them both in water and in air."

I'd rather stare at yours. I couldn't stop looking at his own huge, beautiful eyes.

And then a big white fluffy towel hit me in the head.

"I won't look," he said, already turning back to the kitchenette.

I smiled and hesitated only a minute before slipping out of my clothes and wrapping the huge towel around myself twice. Then I curled up on the couch and tried to keep my eyes open. I figured I wouldn't be very romantic when I was snoring, and I was determined to remember this night for the rest of my life (or at least long enough to recount to Rosie).

Rory appeared in front of me. "You know there's a bed," he said.

"I think that would be tempting fate, Mr. O'Brien," I said.

"Whatever you say, Miss Manchester." He disappeared into the bedroom and returned a moment later with a pillow and a blanket. "Lift your head."

He slipped the pillow under my wet head and spread the blanket around me. As he leaned over to tuck the blanket around me, I grabbed his shirt. I held it for a moment before he took the initiative and bent down to kiss me. It was soft, comforting.

He finally pulled away.

"Where are you going to sleep?" I asked.

"I think it's the gentlemanly thing to offer to sleep on the floor, but since there's an open bed …"

I laughed. "I have a better idea." I lifted the blanket for him to join me on the couch.

"You're so kind, saving me the trouble of having to sleep on the floor or that wonderful, empty, king-size bed." He slipped in beside me. We had to lay on our sides to both fit. Our faces touched on the pillow.

"Are you all right now?" he asked.

I nodded into his forehead. A sob got choked in my throat and I laughed, shaking my head. "At least I thought so." He slipped an arm under my neck and rolled me into his chest. The gesture made me want to sob. "What am I going to do?" I said.

"What do you want to do?" he asked.

"I want to stay here forever."

"Nobody ever wants summer to end," he agreed.

"No," I said. "I want the summer to end. I want everyone in the big houses to go home. I want to stay; I want to see what Oyster Beach looks like in the winter."

"Then do it," he said after a thoughtful pause.

"I can't. I don't have any money."

"Get a job," he said simply.

"Where? I don't know if you've noticed, but I'm not exactly qualified for much."

"Lucky for you, not many qualifications are needed for cleaning cabins or serving burgers on Main Street. But I can tell you, it's not all it's cracked up to be." He was smiling. "You can ask any of the O'Brien kids about that."

"It's got to be better than going back with *them*," I said instead.

"Cora, what do you *really* want?" he said. "You don't really want to stay in Oyster Beach. That's just a form of running away, which is preferable to going home for you. But you've gotta think about what you *really* want. From what I know of you, you don't want to run away. You want to find something. Your life. But you've got to think about what that means. Where that is."

I was silent for a long time. I could feel him relaxing, his breathing becoming more regular.

"How did you know you should go to Ireland?" I finally asked.

I thought maybe he hadn't heard me. I was about to check to see if he was asleep when he finally replied, "I didn't. It was just an idea. An idea that wouldn't get out of my head until I tried it. But I was never sure it was what I *should* do. I'm still not sure. In fact, when I met you, Oyster Beach regained a lot of its old luster."

I leaned back so that I could look him in the face. "So why are you going?" I asked.

"Are you asking me to stay?" he said.

"Are you saying you would stay if I asked you?" I said.

We were looking each other in the eyes, but he was the one that finally backed down with a small laugh. "No, I don't think so," he said. "We're eighteen. I believe what's meant to happen will happen."

I looked at the cabin wall. Decorated with gaudy prints of birds and pheasants. "I don't think I buy that," I said. "That only leads to a life of idleness. I've been waiting for things to happen all my life. I don't want to do that anymore."

We lapsed into another silence.

"Let's not talk about the future anymore," I finally said. I burrowed down beneath the blanket. He pulled his arm out from under my head to dig something out of his pocket. It was the tin whistle.

It reminded me instantly of my conversations with Mr. Hall. I wanted to tell Rory everything I'd heard, every single thing Mr. Hall had said, but it seemed too big for me to get my words around. And I was way too scared to broach the topic of his own mysterious parentage. I finally ventured forth with, "I never knew her first name."

"What?"

"Mrs. O'Leary. I never knew her first name was Lia."

"Yeah, short for Cordelia. But everyone always called her Mrs. O'Leary, for as long as I can remember. Even Mr. O'Leary."

"You knew him," I said, as I watched his fingers deftly twirl the whistle around themselves.

"Yeah, but I was just a little kid when he died. He taught me to play this"—he indicated the whistle—"but I don't remember him much."

"The way Mr. Hall tells it, Mr. O'Leary sounds kind of mean."

Rory shrugged. "He really loved her, and she loved him. But sometimes that isn't enough."

Love not enough? This struck me the wrong way. "When isn't that enough?" I asked.

He thought about this. "Well, when somebody belongs somewhere …" He struggled with his words. "I guess you just have to be where you belong … Mrs. O'Leary never felt like she belonged here in Oyster Beach."

"That sounds just like … she told me something once," I said.

"Oh yeah? She tends to do that a lot." He was trying to lighten the mood.

I smirked. "I mean something that didn't ring true to me."

"Yes, that is odd, her stories are always so realistic."

I laughed outright. "You know what I mean! She seems so open and accepting of everyone—and everything. But then one day she told me, completely seriously, she said, that we need to let things be in their places. Even me. That everything has a place."

"I think so, too."

I looked up at him seriously. "That doesn't make sense. That just sounds like an opportunity to tell people to go back to where they came from. Doesn't that mean I shouldn't be here?"

"Oh, Cora," he sighed, his eyebrows scrunched up. "Where you belong is not necessarily where you came from. It's wherever you *want* to be. That's where your place is." He paused, still flipping the whistle absently. "And I don't think our place is always where we expect it to be."

I moved my cheek to his chest and thought about his words. Maybe I'd misunderstood Mrs. O'Leary. She wasn't telling me I belonged with Owen Carlton and other heirs, she was telling me I needed to figure out where I felt I belonged.

I fell asleep to the sound of the tin whistle and the feeling of Rory breathing, his chest rising and falling below my cheek as he tried to play quietly.

Seid Seamus
SEAMUS'S SHED

T HE NEXT MORNING, RORY WOKE ME UP BY gently kissing my forehead.

"No," I moaned. "I want to sleep."

"We have to get up now; I have to go to work."

Work. The Ritzes. My stomach plummeted from whatever glorious dream I'd been in.

He set about tidying everything and returning things back to their proper places, just how we'd found it, while I put my damp clothes back on. Then he went to the front office, replacing the key ring and dumping the wet towels in a big bin. Nobody was there manning the desk yet.

Really dodged a bullet there, I thought. I couldn't imagine facing kindly Mrs. O'Brien with tousled hair and rumpled, barely dry clothes. Talk about the walk of shame.

"You want to see Mr. O'Leary's shed?" Rory asked.

I hesitated only a moment at the thought of running

into one of the Ritzes. I nodded and felt high as a million clouds as we walked down the boardwalk hand-in-hand. I defied a Ritz to say anything about this—or the boy I was holding hands with. I secretly hoped someone from the big houses would see me as I walked into the Ritz yard with the hired help.

But no one was around. Mr. O'Leary's shed was near the back of the property, a dark, one-room, wooden building. There were a few roof tiles missing; it was obvious this little building hadn't been kept up—the inhabitant had probably always been too busy keeping up the rest of the property to work on his own little corner of it.

Rory led me inside, where four bare walls stood over a sea of boxes. There was a high wooden counter that ran the length of the room, a mess of tools and things spread along it. There were nails all over the wall above it, but all were empty now. Opposite the counter there was a group of iron chairs and a workbench arranged in a circle. And boxes—boxes everywhere.

"What are the chairs for?" I said.

"This was like his den," Rory explained. "He used to have company here. His friends, like Mr. Hall, and townspeople would visit. He had all kinds of stuff here—not just work stuff. And it was decorated and everything." He paused and gestured toward the door. "There were posters all around there. And he kept a lot of personal stuff here. I don't know why he wouldn't keep it at home. Like these animal skins." He picked something leathery up from a big wooden trunk that was under the counter. "There's another smaller one just like it. Mr. Hall said there used to be three, but one was lost a long time ago. They were Mr. O'Leary's most prized possessions—worth a lot, I guess." He put it back and picked up a big knot of fishing wire. "He kept a lot of his fishing collection here, too. This, on the other hand, can't be worth anything." He dropped the tangle back into the trunk. "I think this was his home away from home."

"Did Mrs. O'Leary ever come here?" I asked.

Rory shrugged. "I don't know; I doubt it. I think it was kind of his place to get away from everything at home. He used to bring Aidan and me here when we were kids. But I don't remember ever seeing her here."

I gazed thoughtfully around, trying to imagine what it must have looked like, what it must have been for the mysterious fisherman. If the Ritzes ever appeared here to give instructions, orders. I somehow doubted that a Ritz would step foot in here. He brought Aidan and Rory here, but none of the other O'Brien children? They were younger than the rest, it made sense. But the things Mr. Hall had implied wouldn't leave me, either. I wondered if Mr. O'Leary had been in here shortly before his boat went down. Maybe it was the last place he was—collecting his fishing stuff before departing. Never to return.

"Anyway, I'll be done here in a few days," Rory said. "I'm going through everything. Broken stuff gets tossed in a pile for Mr. Hall to look at. Everything else boxed up, cleaned up, moved out."

"Moved out where? Who's taking all his stuff?" I asked.

Rory shrugged. "Somebody suggested selling it." He put a foot on the big wooden trunk. "There's gotta be a fortune's worth of junk in here. Mrs. O'Leary could use the money. She doesn't seem interested in any of this stuff, but who couldn't use extra cash?" He threw me a glance. "Well, you know what I mean …"

But it made me uneasy. Mrs. O'Leary had money stuffed in books in her little house. Who knew how much of it. Did she really need the money? What would she need it for? Apparently Rory didn't know about the stashed cash.

"So will I see you tonight?" Rory broke into my thoughts.

I grinned. "Only if you want to."

He didn't answer, but slipped his arms around my waist and kissed me. Then he pulled away. "I think I do," he said.

I headed for the door. "Meet me somewhere at eight?"

"The jetty?"

"Of course."

It wasn't until I was outside the Pink Palace, shoes in hand, last night's damp clothes smelling a bit like must, that I realized I was in for round two. *My parents.* It had been a long time since we'd had a fight of this magnitude. This time, I was determined not to give in as easily as I usually did. This was about the rest of my life. I took a deep breath and began to climb the back stairs.

But I was wrong. When I passed my father in the kitchen, he didn't say a word to me. He may have been giving me the silent treatment, but it wasn't a whole lot different than our day-to-day interaction. In the living room, Mom was suspiciously quiet, lifting a few fingers in greeting. That could only mean that the wrath of my father was still on its way.

I stayed carefully away from them, and the next day, I was too consumed in my own world to notice whether my father was talking to me. I had big plans with Rory.

I slipped out of the Pink Palace around nine that evening and met him at the resort.

He was sitting on the edge of the pool, watching his brother Aidan clean the water with a net on a long pole. The pool was closed. We'd purposely waited until after dark when it closed to resort guests. There was just a sliver of the moon out tonight; it lent an eerie effect to the reflections on the water's surface. Almost sinister. But that interpretation was probably produced more by my imagination than any grounding in reality.

Rory jumped up when he heard my footsteps on the boardwalk.

"Hey!" he said brightly. "Come meet my brother Aidan."

"We met briefly," I said, putting on as friendly a face as I could. It probably wasn't very convincing, considering the nerves that were clenching my stomach.

"Hi," Aidan said. As I'd noticed before, he was a mini Rory. Only a bit shorter and with slightly darker hair. And, of course, he was considerably quieter. I found myself wondering which brother was more like Mr. O'Leary.

Rory was beaming, but Aidan and I were both clearly out of things to say. I watched Aidan pull the pole apart and stow it in a wooden cabinet at the side of the pool. *Seriously the polar opposite of Rory.* They were twins to the eye, but he was the introverted, quiet opposite to Rory's friendly exuberance. Who must their mother have been to produce such similar, yet strikingly different boys?

"Thanks, for, uh, cleaning the pool," I said lamely.

Jesus, shut up, I chided myself. *He's not the pool boy*. Well, technically, he may have been. But *God* he had Rory's eyes—the same exact big, round, brown eyes.

Aidan nodded absently. "Good luck," he murmured before disappearing into the resort office. I blushed profusely. How embarrassing to be known as the girl who couldn't swim. He could probably swim every bit as well as his older brother. His older brother who was already getting into the pool.

"Come on!" he called happily.

It looked cold. But that was a lame excuse. I finally settled on, "Rory, I'm kinda scared." *And not completely comfortable in a swimming suit*, but I wasn't about to admit that out loud.

He waded to the side of the pool and held his hand out to me. "Sit down."

I pulled off my shorts and t-shirt and unconsciously hunched over, shrinking into myself. What happened to that confident, flirty girl in the Ritz pool? *She's definitely gone.*

I sat down on the side of the pool, lowering my feet in with a gasp. It was, indeed, cold. I took his hand, goose bumps running up my arms and legs.

"You have nothing to worry about; you've got the best teacher in Oyster Beach," he said.

I nodded. I was full of a thousand emotions and I didn't know which one was evident on my face. I was scared, of course; my mother's irrational fear of losing another loved one to the mysterious power of water had definitely had a dark effect on me. I was embarrassed, too, not just to be in a swimming suit in front of this gorgeous boy, but to not know something so typically childish. And I was angry. I was angry at *her* for messing this all up for me. Gretel. She was nothing to me, not even a real person, but she'd caused so much pain. If she hadn't gotten into that pool and drowned, who knows what would be different now? I certainly wouldn't be in this position. Maybe we wouldn't even be at the beach. Maybe my mom wouldn't have been such a tight ball of nerves and generally crazy for the entirety of my life. And I would have had a sister. A small pang pricked at my tummy. She had never been a real person to me. *But she could have been. She* should *have been.*

"You ready to get in?" Rory said.

"How about you swim a little first?" I tried to stall. "Just so I can see what it's supposed to look like," I added lamely.

"I think you've seen me swim enough, it's your turn to try."

I looked at him sharply. Were we finally going to broach the subject of my—well—those mornings at the pier? "You … ?"

He let my unfinished question fall to oblivion. His face said it didn't matter; my face was undoubtedly saying I was confused. His hand in mine felt like electricity as I remembered those mornings back when I didn't know him. It had been a long time since I'd thought of that time; it felt so unnatural to remember a time when I didn't know Rory.

"So, are you ready to get in?" he repeated.

I took a deep breath and nodded.

He put his hands on my hips and lifted me into the pool, pulling me slowly through the water. It was like flying, fluttering free through the water, yet held so firmly to him.

He stopped in the middle, standing up, but my feet just barely grazed the bottom. I wouldn't let go of his hand. We had a long night ahead of us.

"We'll start with floating," he said.

We were wrapped in the same towel, perched on a lounge chair and kissing softly when Aidan appeared again.

I jumped up, self-consciously pulling the towel around me. Rory laughed as my flustered reaction pulled the fluffy towel off his shoulders. God he was hot when his hair was wet and sticking up in all directions after he rubbed it with the towel (and my fingers may have contributed a bit, too). It also helped, of course, that he wasn't wearing a shirt.

I grabbed my clothes and tried to pull them on without letting the towel fall. My suit was still damp but I was too embarrassed to even look Aidan in the face, much less strut around in a swimming suit.

"What's up?" Rory asked him.

"Mom's looking for you," he said. He eyed me struggling awkwardly with the towel and my t-shirt. "And she wants to know who you're with."

"I—we've—I've met your mom," I stammered.

"I'll be right in," Rory told Aidan.

Aidan grinned and left.

Maybe I wasn't an Olympic swimmer. And maybe we'd spent more time kissing than actually practicing swimming. But maybe that was all I needed. The pool wasn't a sinister thing anymore, not after the night I'd just had in it. It would forever be associated with Rory's hands and his laugh.

"Meet me at the pier tomorrow?" I asked as I left.

"Always," he said.

I passed Aidan near the office on my way out. He barely looked up from the book he was reading by the beam of a porch light. I hesitated; my instinct was to say something but he seemed more like the type of person who was a lot happier with as little conversation as possible. A little like me.

I finally resolved on a simple, "Bye."

"Maybe next time you guys will actually get around to swimming."

I grinned. He was all jokes. Maybe he wasn't so different from Rory, after all.

Ag Briseadh Isteach agus ag Briseadh Amach
BREAKING IN AND BREAKING OUT

PRINCESS WAS THE ONLY ONE THAT JUMPED UP TO greet me when I walked in the door. Granted, she was the only one to ever jump up to sniff my shoes, but the silence was alarming that night. Maybe they had been sitting there in the dining room in perfect chilled silence the whole evening, or maybe they'd seen me coming, but that's how both my mother and father were when I entered.

And then I realized they weren't alone. Captain Harville was there, standing awkwardly between them by the table.

He looked about to speak, but throwing a glance at my parents, he realized the delinquent wasn't to be treated with congeniality. Instead he just nodded a quick hello. He looked extremely uncomfortable.

"Hi," I said brightly, hoping to break the tension.

"Where have you been?" Dad said by way of a response.

"I was just—"

"We don't need to talk about that," Mom said gently. "Right now." She took a calming breath. "Captain Harville came to speak with you."

"It needn't sound as formal as all that," Captain Harville said. He held his hat in his hand and twisted it nervously. "There was a break-in down at the Ritzes' and I was just doing the rounds of everybody who may know something, may have seen anything unusual around the Ritz house recently."

I froze. *A break-in?* Had someone seen us at their pool? We'd left everything exactly the way we'd found it. But it was still trespassing.

"When did it happen?" I said, willing my voice not to break.

"Last night."

I let out a deep breath, willing my cheeks to go back to their normal color. We'd been nowhere near the Ritz house last night. "Oh, I'm sorry, I don't know anything. I don't hang out with the Ritz kids anymore."

"That's not why he's here," Dad cut in sharply. "Actually that's exactly why he's here. As a matter of fact, if you were friendly with that family, he wouldn't be here at all. He's here because you're so damned friendly with that handyman Ritz hired."

"That has nothing—"

"Officer, what was it that was broken into, exactly?" Dad said pointedly.

"Well, it was the little shed at the back of the property. Where the

O'Brien boy works. He wasn't working at the time, though, so I'm sure—"

"Rory?" I nearly yelled. "You think *Rory* did this?" This was directed at my father whose glare hadn't left me, searching for any break in my defense. But it was Captain Harville that cut in quickly.

"Now, nobody's pointing fingers at anybody. It wasn't a serious affair. The door was broken open and there were some things thrown around. Nothing's missing. We're just seeing if anybody knows anything. No harm done."

I looked at my father. He obviously thought there was *much* harm done.

"Well I can promise you neither Rory nor I had anything to do with it," I said firmly.

"That's just fine, and now I'm going to leave you all and I want you to forget I was here. No harm done." Captain Harville hesitated before nodding politely.

Mom got up to show him to the door, but Captain Harville hesitated again in the doorway. "Cora—I also wanted you to know that … well, old Mrs. O'Leary talks about you a great deal. She sure cares for you a whole lot. And she's been real sick lately. Won't you go and see her when you can?"

My heart plummeted and shame flooded my cheeks. That was the second warning I'd gotten about Mrs. O'Leary's health. *How selfish could I possibly be?*

But Dad succeeded in making me look like an angel in comparison just then. "I'm afraid Cora won't have time for that," he said coldly.

"And why's that?" I demanded, spinning to face him.

Dad didn't look up as he said, "Your mother and I have decided it's best if we get everything in order and leave the ninth."

All thoughts in my head came screeching to a halt. "That's only a few days," I said.

"We'll start packing the house up tomorrow," Dad said. Mom was quiet, watching the conversation between the two of us, and throwing awkward glances at Harville. The last thing she wanted was a public brawl. That would set *all* the ladies talking.

"Fine," I said, moving to go upstairs.

"You'll want to say your good-byes to Owen Carlton soon," he said, pronouncing the name carefully. "We'll need you to stay around here, helping get things in order."

I stopped and spun around. "No worries, *father!* I said good-bye to that piece of scum a while ago. He was only trying to get in my pants!"

I stormed up the stairs as my dad stammered for clarification. Mom looked horrified, and Captain Harville, well, his face looked quite alarmed, though I couldn't help thinking I caught a passing glance of amusement there, too.

Early the next morning, there was a soft knock on my door. It brought me out of the dreary in-between state where sleep meets the waking hours. As it was not in either of my parents' natures to do anything softly, I was quite confused as I called, "Come in."

To my great surprise, it was my mom. She came in silently and sat down on the foot of my bed. "Cora, I'm sorry," she said without preamble.

I was flabbergasted. Of all the ways I imagined the next few days would unfold, that was certainly not in any of them. "For—for what?" I stammered.

She seemed to think for a long moment. "This whole summer was supposed to be about healing. And being together and just—just … being *better*." She anxiously ran her hand across the palm of her other hand. "I thought it was my last chance to—you know—fix things. Before you grew up. And left us. It was supposed to heal us all. But it just seems to have broken things more."

Well there it was. Finally in the open. Formulated into a real thought and put into words to stand in our memories forever. How had I imagined I would respond if this topic ever came up between the two of us? So many different ways, but I couldn't remember any of them now. "Mom," I said gently, "I didn't need healing."

"I know," she said, her voice nasally, as if holding off tears. "But I did."

Like so many other times that summer, Mrs. O'Leary came unbidden to my mind. I had never talked to my mother like I had talked to Mrs. O'Leary. Why had I never talked to my mom like that?

"Why didn't you say anything?" I said. "Why whisk us off without explanation?"

"Talking is my strong suit, but communicating? Nobody in this family is very good at that." She paused. "Cora, you're my only girl. I always thought I'd have four girls—all beautiful, and smart, and kind. Maybe one would be an artist. And one an athlete. And—And … But then, when we lost her … and you were the only one to follow—and I got all I wanted in one little girl—but I—I don't know …"

She seemed lost for words, so I offered up my own. "Every parent is guilty of living vicariously through their children," I said.

She shook her head. "That's not it. I've just—I've been keeping things from you for so long, it feels natural. I tell myself I'm just trying to protect you, but in reality, I was just always trying to protect myself."

"What do you mean?"

She sniffed and her eyes welled up for a moment. But then she blinked and they cleared and she went on in a more determined voice. "I knew talking about her wouldn't bother you; you never knew her. But it would hurt me. It would hurt me so much. And it would hurt your dad. We always said we wouldn't talk about it with you so that it wouldn't disturb you or upset you. But it's just like a fairytale, isn't it? A story. You wouldn't have been affected. The ones who would hurt were *us*."

I was quiet for a moment. Mrs. O'Leary was weighing heavily on my mind. *The kappas.* The creatures that pulled children down to drown.

The old woman had said: "I sometimes wonder … what must it be like for the human mother that never sees her child return from the ocean."

How heavy my heart felt, remembering those words. Even when she'd said them, I obviously hadn't comprehended them. Not then.

Only now did I begin to wonder it myself. *What must it have been like?* My poor, poor mother.

The guilt of never having considered my mother's point of view welled up and spilled over in the form of a confession.

"Mom, I-I never went to swimming lessons. This summer, I mean. I went to one lesson and then—well I didn't go in. And I never went back."

"I know that," she said with a weak attempt at a smile.

I was surprised. It wasn't like my mother to know something like that and not confront me with it. "I'm sorry," I finally said.

She took my hand and squeezed it then. We weren't the hugging type. In fact, a hug would have made us both uncomfortable. "I should've sent you when you were a child," she said, shaking her head.

"I went, once. Remember?"

"God, you remember that?" She shook her head. "Joan knew how to raise you better than I did. I was so eager to be a better mother the second time around—not make the same mistakes, even the little ones—that I couldn't see at all how to do it right."

"Mom," I said hesitantly. Mrs. O'Leary's words again rushed into my consciousness, a heady encouragement:

" ... Every mother feels the tiniest bit of pride in her child ... I think of Ronan and I am more proud of anyone else in the world." Just what I needed to make the bigger confession. I took a deep breath. "Mom, I didn't get in to Western."

"Well, there's a wait list, maybe—"

"No," I interrupted. "I didn't get a spot on the wait list. I got rejected. At the beginning of the summer. I got a letter. I didn't tell anyone."

She looked at me for a long moment. Her face revealed that we were at another point where Joan would have been far more capable of maneuvering the high tides of emotion.

"That's okay," she finally murmured. "We'll figure something out."

And I didn't argue. I didn't yell at her that I didn't want her to "figure something out"—that *I* needed to figure it out. I was suddenly, for the first time in my life, positive that we could get it right this time. I could get it right this time—and whether my mother liked it or not, she would always love me. Just like another mother I knew.

"Do you—" I faltered. "Do you still need healing?"

Mom sighed and patted my hand. "That's not for you to worry about, honey. I'll find it. It was silly to think it was here." She gestured around her at the walls and furniture and suddenly fell to laughing. "It *is* pink, isn't it?"

I laughed outright. The first time I'd had a real laugh with my mother in a long, long time.

"It wasn't a silly idea," I said. "Coming here. It was wonderful." I paused, knowing that if I proposed what I was thinking, we would have turned a corner in our relationship from which there was no retreating behind our emotional blockades. We'd already come so far, so I decided to barge ahead. "Mom, do you want to meet one of my new friends?"

My tennis shoes knew the way to the little yellow house without direction.

Mrs. O'Leary wasn't on the porch. When I knocked on the door, it was a good four or five minutes before she answered. She looked quite shaken up when she saw me, but then she saw my mother behind me and her face grew softer, kinder.

"Cora," she said, studying my mother, "you brought a friend."

"Mrs. O'Leary, this is my mom," I said.

The little old woman came outside, shutting the front door behind her. "How do you do, dear?" she said, as she moved to her big rocking chair.

I wanted to get straight to the point of our visit, before I lost the courage with this idea of mine. Before I convinced myself that putting two slightly crazy people together was a terrible idea. "Mom, Mrs. O'Leary lost her husband at sea."

My mom's face looked pained for the old woman and I wondered if this was a bad idea.

"Cora told me that your firstborn drowned," Mrs. O'Leary said simply. "You poor child."

My doubt cleared. I was relieved that she had gotten the point so quickly. I studied the old woman's face as her eyes characteristically roved the ocean. She certainly didn't look as sick as everyone had been telling me she was.

"Do come sit," she said. I started to move to the chair before I realized she was speaking to my mother. Mom sat awkwardly down on the chair, and Mrs. O'Leary took her hand.

"Cora, why don't you stroll and come back for your mother in a bit?"

"Okay," I said, looking at my mother for verification that this wouldn't alarm her. But she was looking intently at Mrs. O'Leary, who had begun to expound on the good qualities of her Seamus.

I left them and found myself winding toward the red cabins before thinking better of it. I didn't want to seem overbearing, he could be working, and we didn't have plans, so I made a move to turn around—but not before I spotted Jen.

I froze, a chill running up my neck.

She was standing in the middle of the boardwalk near the resort office, with her big blonde hair, and her tan arms were wrapped around Rory's neck. God, she was skinny. His arms were around her, too. Limply, but they were there. On her back.

It was just a hug, I told myself. But to the other part of me, that tiny (or not-so-tiny) insecure part of me, it looked like a passionate embrace.

Well, you're just as crazy as the two ladies back on the porch, I told myself. I turned around too quickly to see how long it lasted. I went to the beach and walked up and down in the sand for a while, actively trying to think of anything but that image that just didn't seem to want to go. I don't know how long I stayed there, digging my toes into the sand and then kicking it up around me.

Eventually, I despondently made my way back to Mrs. O'Leary's, not knowing if it was too early to return, but I had nowhere else to go. And I didn't have the heart to wander. I was too busy mustering all my strength to prove to myself that I wasn't heartbroken—that I was relaxed. Easygoing. It hadn't bothered me. But I was a stubborn person to convince; it wasn't working.

When I first glimpsed my mother's face again, she was smiling. A soft, gentle smile, full of emotion. When she saw me, the smile grew harder, more forced. It was obvious they had been talking about me. Mom said good-bye to Mrs. O'Leary slowly, but I didn't interrupt them. They clasped hands for a few moments, and Mrs. O'Leary waved good-bye to me. She moved to her house without saying anything else.

As we walked home, Mom didn't tell me what had been said that day, what the two ladies had told each other, but she did take my hand. And she didn't let it go until we climbed the back steps of the Pink Palace.

I didn't go to the jetty to meet Rory that night.

Brí an Fhocail
THE MEANING OF THE WORD

I T WOULD BE A COP OUT TO SAY I DIDN'T GO TO
the pier because of my mother—because I didn't
want to displease her. That's what I told myself, but at that
point, I firmly believed that after talking to Mrs. O'Leary,
my mom would leave that summer feeling content no
matter what I did.

In the end, I was too scared to even look at Rory, who
inspired deeper and more complex thoughts and feelings
in me than any other person I'd ever met. I was so full, I
felt that I would spill over. And thinking about Jen
hugging him, that was a conversation that would definitely
make me spill over. And I wasn't sure I could handle it.

The next morning, I decided I should go and say my
own good-bye to Mrs. O'Leary. I was afraid of how she
would react. Everyone had been telling me how sick she
was, and I wasn't sure how important I was to her—but if

Captain Harville was to be believed, I mattered. I was afraid to upset her, but at the same time I knew it would be worse to go see her once more without mentioning my leaving, only to never return. The loneliness I felt surrounding and suffocating that little yellow house ached inside me, even from as far away as the Pink Palace.

I set out, going over in my head what I would say to her. But I never made it that far. I ran smack dab into someone on the boardwalk. Literally.

"I'm sorry," I said, backing away, "I—" But my apology died away as soon as I realized who it was.

I felt no urge to punch her. Or slap her. Or even do the cowardly thing and call her a bitch. All I felt was the overwhelming yearning to go shake her hand. All bets off. All hard feelings gone. *You win.*

Of course I didn't do any of that. We eyed each other awkwardly, but it was too late to pretend we hadn't seen each other. To pretend we weren't thinking who-knows-what about each other. There were hard emotions in her eyes, probably a reflection of my own.

And as I stood there, having worked so hard since yesterday to banish Rory from my thoughts—as I stood there, groping for something to say to her, I realized she didn't look angry or bitchy or anything like my rival. She looked sad. Inexpressibly sad.

With the boy forced out of my mind, I could, for the first time, look at her like another girl. A little girl who, the first time I had met her months ago, had obviously just finished crying. A little girl whose big brother had just died. A little girl who was probably having the worst summer of her life.

"Jen," I said, willing my voice not to break. "I'm really sorry about your brother. And anything I may have said that made you feel sad." *Great, that was on par with a kindergartner's apology.* I wasn't exactly great at expressing myself, but she nodded, so some kind of point was getting across.

"I can't even imagine losing someone like that. And at sea. I can't begin to fathom how you feel. But I know it's ten times greater than any pain I've ever felt." I imagined my mother's face. The times I'd walked in on her talking to a friend or my dad about *her.* The tears, the confusion, the trying to hide it all behind a smile. A pain greater than I'd ever felt. Always protecting Cora. Protecting Cora from feeling a pain that monstrous. "I'm really sorry," I said again. My eyes welled up in spite of myself.

Jen sniffed. I looked up to see her eyes welling, too. Just as I began to wonder if she was going to respond at all, she murmured, "Thanks, Cora." It was almost a whisper. But it was enough.

In an unconsciously mutual agreement, we turned our opposite ways down the boardwalk. Once I had turned away I was able to stop the tears. But I was certainly not fit to see Mrs. O'Leary. I would go see her tomorrow.

With my mother's recent reconciliation and Jen's grief on my mind, emotions I couldn't control were raging through me as I walked home. I'd made it right with so many people, but there was another that I knew I had to get out of the way.

I wiped my nose on my sleeve and called Rosie. She picked up with a "Heya, bitch!"

I responded with: "You made me feel like boyfriends were more important than me."

Of course, the other end of the line went silent. It was quiet for a long time but I didn't hang up. "I'm sorry," she finally said.

"It's okay," I said. "I think I'm okay with it now. But you always put boys before me. As if having a boyfriend was more important than having a best friend." I paused for breath. And, more importantly, courage. "Eventually I started to believe it. I wanted a boyfriend just for the sake of having one, because I admired you so much. And ... well, I was jealous."

"Cora, you were always more important than any boy." Her voice was deep and full of emotion. Unlike the flippant tone she usually had in all of our conversations.

"Well, thanks. I guess I needed to hear it." I paused. "And I know that one day I won't be. One day there will be a boy that sticks around or that you *let* stick around, and he will become more important in your life than me. And that's how it's supposed to be. I'm okay with that—"

"But that hasn't happened yet," Rosie interrupted. "We'll cross that bridge when we come to it."

I laughed. "Okay."

There was silence as I tried to climb out of the pit of emotions we were stuck in.

I lightened my tone. "In other news, I have a huge crush on a boy."

"Not that it's the most important thing in the world, but ..." Rosie tried to keep her voice casual. "But tell me *all* about it!"

I couldn't suppress my giggles.

When I opened the screen door to the back porch at the Pink Palace, I got—despite what this summer had been—one of the biggest shocks yet. The tiny white iron table was surrounded by both my parents, looking highly uncomfortable and confused, and *Rory*.

I stuttered many unintelligible things before my dad said, "Cora, this young man has been waiting for you for quite a while."

Everything relating to Jen or Rosie or Mrs. O'Leary was gone. Once again, I was selfishly lost in my own world. And this one was unfathomably uncomfortable. "I—I—this is Rory," I stammered.

"We've met," Dad said coolly.

Rory looked uneasy, but not quite so shaken up as either of my parents. Dared I imagine he was the tiniest bit amused?

I desperately tried to gather my thoughts into the same hemisphere. "We're going to go for a walk," I said to my parents. "I'll be right back." And I turned on my heel and walked back down the porch steps without so much as a glance at Rory. But I heard him scrambling down the steps after me. I hadn't even cleared the landing before he began.

"I'm sorry, I didn't mean to make them mad—or you—Cora stop."

But I kept walking toward the boardwalk.

"You didn't leave me any choice," he went on. "You didn't show up last night, and I don't even have your number for Christ's sake."

I kept walking, but slowed down to let him catch up. I was going to make up some bullshit story about how my crush had dissipated, but it was so far from the truth that I couldn't even say it out loud.

"Cora, Captain Harville said your family had decided to leave early, and—Jesus—Cora, I thought you guys had gone. I thought I'd never see you again!" He drew me to him, his arms squeezing me tightly. I stood there limply, not reacting. He pulled away. "What's going on?"

"You should be with Jen," I finally said.

"*What?*" he sputtered.

"I was on my way to meet you yesterday, but I saw you guys together, and … Rory I saw you with her. She's … she's pretty and she's like you. And I just saw her, like five minutes ago …" I trailed off; I didn't want to go there. Of all the things going wrong in that girl's life, losing her friend or crush or whatever he was to her didn't seem fair. "And she's, she's used to this place. It's best if I just bow out now— and I'm not angry—I'm not upset—but we've been acting crazy. I have to leave, like, the day after tomorrow. That night at the resort was crazy. She's … Jen's right for you."

Rory's face looked furious. "And I don't get a say in this?" he demanded. "Cora, I was saying good-bye to Jen. I'm leaving, too, remember? I've known Jen for a long time. I know she's had crushes on me from time to time, but she deserved an explanation as to why I was disappearing from her life so suddenly. With only a few weeks left to hang out, I've virtually disappeared from her life. She needed an explanation. And she got it. I told her that I was strangely and ridiculously and foolishly and oddly, prematurely in love with you."

I gulped. "I—well—" I fell back into silence. *What in the hell do I say to that?* But he wasn't going to say anything more so I had to come up with something fast. "Mrs. O'Leary doesn't even think humans are capable of real love," I said.

What? What a strange thing to say! Stop talking!

"I don't know what love is," I added with a squeak.

A normal boy would have excused himself then on the mere fact that I was bat-shit crazy. But not Rory. He just laughed. "I don't think anyone knows what love is. *Ever.* Instead of waiting my whole life to say it until I know what it is for sure—and risking never actually knowing, well, I'd rather say it every chance I get, instead."

"But everybody means something different when they say it," I protested.

He laughed and pulled me close to him again, cupped my face in his hands.

"Well when I say, I love you, Cora Manchester, it means I'm head over heels for you as much as my schoolboy mind can understand, and I want to spend every waking moment with you until you leave Oyster Beach."

Fan Liom
WAIT FOR ME

RORY FELT LIKE THE BEST FRIEND THAT I'D EVER had. He was quiet when I wanted to talk and he was talkative when I wanted to listen. And he was oftentimes quiet when I wanted to be quiet. For the first time I understood what maybe, just maybe, Rosie had felt with a few of those boys that she had dated. Certainly not Steve, but maybe the new one. It was the endless talking with Rory and the renewed calls to Rosie and the reinstated attentions from my mom that finally convinced me that I couldn't afford to miss out on any more conversations with my dad.

He was in the living room behind the newspaper when I sat down next to him on the couch.

He looked over the top of the paper at me briefly, as if to verify that I wasn't an intruder. Then he disappeared behind it again. Apparently I was an intruder—to his alone time.

"Dad," I said confidently. I was ready to make some sort of argument to defend my behavior, to try to make him understand everything I was feeling. But he interrupted me.

"Save it, Cora, I've had enough of the serious talking today."

I looked at him quizzically.

He emerged again from behind the paper. "Your mother beat you to it," he said. "I know all about Western and the swimming lessons and everything else."

"I—um, okay." I forgot any piece of the argument I had just been prepared to make.

"Where did you come from?" he said with misty eyes, shaking his head slowly.

My mouth hung open in response. *Clever, Cora, really clever.*

"You're nothing like your mother, and you're nothing like me, that's for damn sure."

"Nothing like you?" I repeated. "Are you kidding?"

He smiled weakly. "I guess there is a bit of your old dad in your attitude. Just the kind of attitude to put at the front of a boardroom."

We lapsed into a silence that almost felt comfortable. I was used to silences with my father. This almost felt natural again.

"We'll figure something out, Cora." He was actually looking at me, holding the newspaper in his lap.

I nodded. It was kind of vague, but it was better than the silent treatment.

When I met Rory that evening at the pier, I don't think there was one second of silence between us. One subject led to the next seamlessly. It was like we were making up for eighteen years of not knowing each other.

It wasn't until I said I should be going home for dinner that we grew quiet. We weren't good at good-byes, perhaps because we knew a giant one was looming in the near future. I hadn't yet gotten up from my spot nestled in his arms.

"Why can't you come to Ireland?" he said softly.

We'd been over this. About a million times. "You know why," I said. My eyes were closed. His voice grew to mythical proportions in the blackness of my mind.

"Cora, it's not about the money, is it?" he said.

I opened my eyes. *How did he know?* I had told him several times that I didn't have any of my own money to spend as I pleased and passed that off as the reason I couldn't come with him to Ireland. But he had somehow read my mind that that wasn't the truth. Not the whole truth. I sat up and looked him in the eyes. He looked back, imploring me to tell him.

"It would kill them," I finally said. "Leaving them would hurt them more than if I refused to go to college for the rest of my life. Their biggest fear is losing another daughter. I'll travel one day—when I have my own money, when they know that I'm not running away, that I'll come back for them."

Rory nodded understandingly and looked out at the ocean. He bore a striking resemblance to Mrs. O'Leary, the steady gaze, trolling the horizon. It shocked me to notice that. Because Mrs. O'Leary was very much not on my mind in those hours with Rory. We wanted to learn everything about each other that we could in the little time we had. So we talked about ourselves—or didn't talk at all—learning about each other in other ways.

When Rory walked me home that night, I invited him inside, to the bowels of the Pink Palace. My parents were already asleep, but I showed him around the embarrassingly pink house—my cheeks to match—and ended up on the balcony off my room.

"It's almost a new moon," he said, putting his hands on the railing on either side of me so that I was enveloped in his arms.

"Spring tide," I said.

"Right!" He was proud. "You've got a great memory. Let's hope you remember me at least … *twice* that long."

This was the last thing I wanted to talk about. "Rory, stop," I whined. I spun around, flustered, only to find myself quite close to his face. This only flustered me further.

He looked down at me, his lips even with the tip of my nose.

"Promise me that you'll come visit."

"My very first paycheck from my very first job, or, uh, ten or thirty paychecks, will go toward the plane ticket," I said with a grin. Though his words were probably just that—words, mine were not a joke. I'd visit him in September if I could. But I knew I'd never be ready by then. I needed money … and courage. "I'd have to save for a … a very long while," I said. *Would you wait for me?*

Rory brushed his lips across my forehead. "Make sure you keep that all in a safe place. A dictionary or two should do the trick."

I looked at him sharply. "So you *do* know she keeps her money in a book?" I laughed, delighted to share the secret at last.

"*A* book?" he repeated. "Try *all* her books. What other use are they when you can't read? I stumbled upon that little gem a few years ago."

"Do you ever steal a dollar or two here or there for the movies or a burger?"

"What?" he laughed loudly. "No! Did you?"

"No!" I laughed and sighed in his arms. "I'll just carve up all my books and stash money in there as it comes. A couple full *Harry Potter* books should get me to Ireland. I might have enough in, well, three or four years."

"So, when you're done with college," he smiled.

"Then I'll have my own small fortune and I can travel the world, or just to Ireland. Provided, of course, that you haven't fallen in love and married some Irish lass by then. Or without the love—you know, for the citizenship."

"I think it's the frat boys at whatever college you end up at that we have to worry about," he said.

"Stop," I pleaded again.

The next day was my last in Oyster Beach. I had only two things to accomplish.

First, to go to the little yellow house and say good-bye to Mrs. O'Leary.

Second, to meet Rory at the pier under a black sky and somehow say good-bye to the first boy I'd ever loved.

D'Fhág Sé
HE LEFT

THE NEXT DAY WAS ONE OF THOSE CHARACTER-istically windy days I'd come to expect from Oyster Beach. A storm threatened to invade from somewhere down the coast and the birds were active in the sky.

Nobody answered the door at the little yellow house when I knocked. I waited for a long time, sitting down on the rocking chair for a bit. I knocked again and then wandered away, not knowing what to do. I had to say good-bye. I wasn't going to leave without seeing her.

I wandered toward the pier out of habit. Or maybe out of some other primal urge.

But as I approached, I discerned a shape at the end of the pier. It was a person. There was somebody standing on our pier, and I knew Rory's figure too well to think that it was him. But I *did* recognize the person ...

"Mrs. O'Leary?" I shouted.

Sure enough, it was the hunched form of the old woman standing on the end of the rocking pier. If her presence there wasn't strange enough, she was acting incredibly suspicious—pacing back and forth, taking a few steps this way, then that, moving about much more than she usually did. The wind whipped at her skirt and at the scarf wrapped around her head. She looked so thin and frail, as though she would flutter away in the slightest breeze, yet these gales seemed to have no effect on her. She should have been torn from her spot and swept away into the water.

Swept away into the water. A chill ran up my spine. That's probably exactly what she wanted. She hobbled back and forth on the end of the pier as it swayed precariously in the waves.

"Mrs. O'Leary!" I called again, taking a few tentative steps from the beach onto the familiar wooden slats.

She twirled around with more energy than I would have expected her capable of. Her eyes took a moment to find me, but when they did, they were wild. I was so used to their calm trolling of the ocean, patient yet eager, that today they looked downright insane.

"Cora," she said excitedly. She moved a few steps toward me and then retreated to her position, looking anxiously over her shoulder at the water.

"Mrs. O'Leary," I gulped, "what's the matter?" I approached her hesitantly. "I was just coming to visit you. But no one was at your house."

I couldn't help noticing what a stark contrast was before me. The Mrs. O'Leary that had soothed my mother—calm, loving and helpful—

to this woman who would paint a not-so-surprising portrait in a mental institution.

"Cora, I couldn't find it." She was wringing her wrinkly, spotted hands.

I thought for a moment. "Your sweater?" I asked.

Mrs. O'Leary looked as though about to burst into tears. She shook her head slowly. "I looked everywhere. I looked in his shed. He hid it, Cora. I loved the man, but he never understood me."

"Who? Mrs. O'Leary, what are you talking about? Why are you out here?"

She just shook her head and looked back out at the ocean, as if expecting to find something there.

"Have you come out here before?" I asked, confused.

"It's my fault," she said. "I chose this life. It's all my own doing. All my fault. Mine. All of it."

This hauntingly echoed things she'd said to me the very first time I'd had a conversation with her on her porch. About leaving her mother. Choosing a different life. It was fine under the comfortable eaves of her porch, but here, in her present state, it unsettled me. "Mrs. O'Leary, let's go inside," I suggested gently.

But she moved away from me, closer toward the edge of the pier. I backed away a few paces, afraid of her falling in. Or, more realistically, *jumping* in.

"Mrs. O'Leary, you can talk to me about it—whatever's bothering you," I said desperately. "Let's just go back to the house."

"I can't find it," she said again, this time softer, as though all hope was gone. "I looked all over that house. I went to his shed."

It took two admissions from her for it to dawn on me. It came washing over me like a tidal wave. "Mrs. O'Leary, *you* broke into the Ritzes'?"

"And it wasn't there. Everything was in boxes."

My mind was reeling. This little old woman was a burglar? I spun through as many ideas to get her away from the water as I could. "Mrs. O'Leary, I think I know who can find it," I said quickly.

I was bluffing. I had no idea who could help her at this point. But I couldn't do this alone. She looked as though she was going to jump right off the end of the pier. Not jump, exactly, but just slip happily away into the waves, and despite my recent pseudo swimming lesson, I would be quite unable to save her then.

She looked at me thoughtfully, as if weighing my merit. "I'm ready to go, Cora."

And I knew she wasn't talking about going back to the house. "I know, Mrs. O'Leary. But first we have to go back to your house. I know who can help."

I repeated the lie, but I didn't know what else to do.

Miraculously, she let me take her arm and lead her back to the boardwalk. She walked slowly and stopped often to look back at the ocean. I let her look; I didn't press her to move on until she was ready, for fear that she might turn back.

When we got to the house I did the only thing I could think of. I didn't know anybody's number in Oyster Beach, but surely 911 could yield some sort of help.

Captain Harville was there within minutes. And he was accompanied by a local doctor.

Mrs. O'Leary was standing quietly in the middle of the living room, staring out the window at the water. She looked frightened when Captain Harville came in.

"What happened?" he asked me.

Mrs. O'Leary looked from the doctor to me with big, round eyes. Somehow, this had been a betrayal. By calling for professional help, I had betrayed her. We both knew that. To avoid the crushed look in her eyes, I turned to Captain Harville and quietly explained to him how I'd found her.

He nodded, and we both watched silently as the doctor gently tried to persuade a protesting Mrs. O'Leary to lie down.

The doctor finally had to take her arm, and though his touch was soft, she reacted violently, jerking her arm free. I tried to tune out her protestations.

"Cora, why don't you go home?" Captain Harville suggested gently.

I would have said no, I would have stayed with her, but I was too scared. *Too weak.* I nodded absently and stumbled outside.

Just because I couldn't be with Mrs. O'Leary didn't mean I wouldn't try to help her. Every time I'd seen her over the past weeks I'd become more and more confused. And there was one person who I was sure knew more than he was letting on.

Not knowing where he lived, I went straight to the antiques shop.

Luckily, it was open, and didn't appear to be busy. I barged in, setting the tiny bell on the door into a frantic high-pitched frenzy. "Why don't you go to see her anymore?" I demanded, bearing down on the counter.

Mr. Hall, turning away from a display case he'd been bent over, looked wildly around the store. Belatedly, I realized there was a little old woman near the back, perusing quilts. But I didn't care.

"She's going crazy all alone in that tiny house, why have you abandoned her?" I demanded again.

Mr. Hall shot another look at the woman, then back at me, begging me to be civil in front of the customer. But the woman seemed to understand a violent argument was looming, and she made a quick exit.

"She needs someone, and you know her the best—"

"Cora," Mr. Hall interrupted. He went to the door and flipped the cardboard sign around to read "closed" to the outside world. I waited for him to explain, taking the moment to catch my breath. But he didn't seem to have anything else to say.

"Well?" I demanded. "You called Seamus your best friend, and he loved her, and you treat her like she's already dead!"

His shoulders seemed to crumple with the weight of the accusation. For the first time I realized how old Mr. Hall must have been. Comparable to Mrs. O'Leary's age, however old that might be. Tall with a thin face and a large pair of round glasses, I'd always seen Mr. Hall as something akin to a professor. But now—now he looked weak, as though he couldn't hold up his head any longer.

"I found her out on the beach just now, pacing and talking nonsense," I said, softer this time.

Mr. Hall's face registered shock. "You found her on the jetty?"

What? I tried to mask the shock on my face. *The jetty?* He said it as if it belonged to someone besides me. Someone besides Rory and me. "How do you know about the jetty?"

Mr. Hall looked me in the eye, once again giving me the feeling that he was sizing me up, deciding what to tell me and what to hide.

"You spend a lot of time with the O'Brien boy," he said.

"So?" I demanded, my anger rising again. "What does that have to do with *anything*?"

"He swims there every morning," Mr. Hall says.

"I know."

He took a deep breath and retreated behind the counter. "Lia used to spend hours upon hours out on that pier. Looking for her little boy. First Ronan—then the second baby."

My blood ran cold. So she had been there before. *How had that never come up in our conversations, this whole summer?* My favorite retreat was Mrs. O'Leary's old stomping ground. A terribly sad, depressing stomping ground.

"People thought she was crazy," Mr. Hall went on. "She'd be out there all day, sometimes all night. Those who thought she'd done it herself, well they thought she was just trying to cover it up. Pretending to search for them. Pretending to mourn. But I always knew she didn't kill them."

My heart was beating so fast, I thought I'd faint. He had come right out and said it. People thought Mrs. O'Leary had murdered her own babies. They thought she was nuts—not because she told fairytales— but because they believed she had drowned her own infant sons.

I could bear it if they thought her stories were insane and the jabber of an unstable woman. *But her own children?* How could they believe that kind, sweet old woman had murdered her own children?

"People will talk about whatever entertains them," Mr. Hall said, as if in response to my thoughts. "There were some who were on her side. But even then, a baby—returning from the ocean? Everyone knew she wasn't right in the head. Seamus paid the best doctors in the area to convince her that the boys were gone. But she never stopped. Whenever Seamus was gone, even after the second child died—in fact, more often after the second child died—she would sneak to the jetty and wait until Seamus went and dragged her back home. After Seamus left, she nearly lived out there. Except those days when she would search that house frantically. She tore it apart from foundation to roof. She would have died on that jetty if we hadn't dragged her back to land to eat every once in a while. I did my fair share of dragging. For years after Seamus left."

I knew Mr. Hall was trying to prove that he *had* cared for Mrs. O'Leary. That he'd done his fair share of watching her. But there was one thing he'd said that blotted out everything else.

"Seamus …" I was nearly speechless. "Seamus *left?*" The room was hot and sticky all of a sudden. I could only whisper. "I thought he was lost at sea."

"Many people do," Mr. Hall said. *Many people.* Including Rory.

"He *left* her?" My initial reaction of a brokenness inside of me was becoming rapidly replaced with anger. It was welling inside me. "You knew that all along? You know her past, you know everything she's been through! Why won't you help her? Stay with her? She's sick, she's not—she doesn't make sense anymore! *Why* do you ignore her?" My hysteria was increasing with each word, quickly reaching an alarming note. "Why, for Christ's sake, *why* won't you help her?"

"Because I promised I wouldn't," Mr. Hall said simply.

The world stopped. Everything was quiet. My mind grasped hopelessly at all the things Mr. Hall had ever told me.

"Promised who?" I spit out, afraid of the answer.

"Seamus. Before he left, he made me promise I wouldn't tell her where to find the skins. I think I was the only one who knew where they were. But even I never learned where the third one was. And then Seamus left and … well, I stayed away."

"Where to find—the—the what?"

"I think Lia has told you what she is," Mr. Hall said, his shrewd eyes squinting behind his glasses, as if to better see into my head. He took a deep breath and went on quickly. "You've heard the legends— what awful pining the women have for the sea. How hard it is on them. But you never hear how hard it is on the man. The man who takes one for his wife. To watch something so natural as a fisherman falling in love with the sea—when it goes wrong, it's painful to watch. After Seamus left, I couldn't stand to see her anymore. I think we're all guilty of that. Not easing someone else's pain because we're afraid it would increase our own."

My own mother had said exactly the same thing to me. But I

couldn't stop to draw conclusions, to make some sense of the disorder in my mind. Mr. Hall was in a kind of frenzy, words spilling from his mouth.

"I thought he was crazy when he told me what she was—what he'd done. But then she became pregnant and I'd never seen two happier people. And that's it, isn't it? What drove them apart in the end. When she told Seamus what she'd done with the children, why, I'd never seen him like that. He was fit to murder."

"What did she do with the children?" I demanded.

"That's why Seamus hid the sealskins in the end," Mr. Hall barreled right on. "After he left, he didn't care if she went back. But he knew she loved those boys. She didn't know where to find the littlest, but her firstborn, she loved from afar. And Seamus knew that if she found her skin and went back, there was nothing that could keep her from taking that boy with her."

I shook my head. *No.* No. "They drowned," I said softly.

Mr. Hall's eyes squinted farther. "They say it's the woman who can't take the yearning for the sea any longer and eventually leaves, but we saw a different story here. The woman, tied to the land, and the man fleeing. Quite the opposite story."

Those unsettling eyes. They were looking at me like that again— like he was taking the measure of my mind. Like he was trying to decipher what I understood. What I'd do. I realized all of a sudden that I'd unconsciously taken a few steps backward. He was waiting to see what I'd do next. *What would I do?* I turned and sprinted out of the shop to the tune of the little bell.

An Selkie
THE SELKIE

I WENT STRAIGHT TO FIND RORY. I FELT WILD, MY heart bumping around inside my chest without control, and I was sure my face looked just the same. *Rory!*

But it was Aidan who I found first.

"Aidan, where's Rory?" I demanded.

"I'll get him."

Thank God for Aidan's disinterest in conversation, I thought. The last thing I could do right now was string together some niceties.

"Rory!" I nearly screamed when he emerged from the resort office.

His face fell when he saw me. "What's the matter?"

"What did you do with the animal skins? The animal skins from Seamus's shed? On the Ritz estate, you showed me an animal skin! That day I went to the shed with you! Where is it?" I knew there were so many things I had to tell him. So many things he didn't know! But I had to find those skins. They belonged to Mrs. O'Leary. I knew nothing would be right until Mrs. O'Leary had them back.

Rory's hands were black with oil and he was trying to wipe his fingers clean with a dirty rag. "I—I gave everything to Mr. Hall that day. The whole trunk. Mr. Hall has it all."

"*Mr. Hall?*"

"I took it down to the antiques shop that afternoon. He said he'd sell it." Rory looked nervous. "He said he'd sell what he could and give the money to Mrs. O'Leary. Why? What's the matter?"

"He had them," I said to myself. "He had them the whole time! He was standing there *talking* to me with them right there in his shop!" What was he planning on doing with them?

I spun around. Aidan stood silently, watching. I just saw the flash of his confused face as I turned on my heel and ran. I ran faster than I'd ever run in my life.

"Cora!" Rory shouted after me.

"I'm sorry!" I spun around and yelled, without stopping. "Just wait here!"

So Mr. Hall had held the skins in his hands as Mrs. O'Leary scrambled through the dark shed on the Ritz estate. He had watched from afar as she scurried around like a criminal. And he had them now. And he'd lied about it. Or had he? I had never thought to ask him if he had them in his possession.

I slammed to a halt at the door to the antiques shop. The closed sign was still up. I banged on the door, but nobody responded. I tugged at the door as hard as I could, but it was locked. There didn't seem to be anyone inside.

I need to find him. I need to find him!

I didn't know what would happen when I did. Would I demand he give her skin to her? Or would I demand he hide it forever? Let her die, an old lady, in peace? I didn't know, but whatever I decided, it would be demanding. I'd had enough of this man and his cryptic loyalty to Seamus. And the other skin … and the one that was lost. Those were for … her sons …

But that didn't make sense! It had been many, many years since Mrs. O'Leary had been young. Her sons would be grown.

But I couldn't think about that now. I had to find those damned skins! It occurred to me then, just like the flick of a switch. What if I was underestimating Mr. Hall? What if …

I ran to Mrs. O'Leary's little yellow house as fast as my legs would carry me. People stared and shot interested glances my way, but I ignored them and ran no matter how my calves ached.

I leaped up the front steps of the little yellow house and banged on the door with both fists and a foot.

Mr. Hall opened it too quickly to have been doing anything other than guarding the door.

"Wh-what are you doing here?" I stuttered. I had this tiny niggling feeling that the man was every bit as ill as Mrs. O'Leary, and though I tried, I couldn't convince myself otherwise. "Where is Mrs. O'Leary?"

His face was calm, serious, but the hint of a smile was on his lips. "She's gone," he said. His eyes didn't leave mine.

"Gone?" I repeated.

Captain Harville appeared then through the narrow arched hallway. My eyes flitted between the two of them. "Where is she?" I asked again, wildly. There was no sign of the doctor from earlier.

"Cora, come inside," Captain Harville said. He spoke carefully and calmly in stark contrast to my inability to control anything—my words, my breathing, my shaking legs. "Cora, she made a will. She left everything to you and Rory."

I didn't know precisely why, but there was a sinking feeling in my stomach. *A will?* "When did she make a will?" *She's known me less than three months.*

"She made it a few weeks ago," Captain Harville said. "She's been ready to go for some time. You know this. I only convinced her to prepare for the … concrete side of things a few weeks ago. I called Rory O'Brien but he wasn't there; I left a message with Aidan. I called your house, too, but you weren't there, of course. Always one step ahead of us." He chuckled softly. "Cora, don't be upset. She was ready to go. She *wanted* to go."

"To go?" I said limply. "You were in on this? I called you here!" I stared at Captain Harville. How much else was going on that I didn't know about? What if this was just the tip of the crazy-freaking iceberg? I couldn't process all this right now! I was supposed to leave Oyster Beach *today*. It was … it was August ninth … it was …

"Spring tide," I said breathlessly.

"I brought her the sealskins," Mr. Hall said. "Right after you came to see me today. It had gone far enough. I haven't always been there for

Lia, but you convinced me that in the end I had to be."

Something still wasn't right.

I felt weak. I needed to sit down. I stumbled to one of the couches and collapsed. A tiny cloud of dust puffed into the air.

"She left you all her books," Captain Harville said softly. "And she left the house to Rory."

"Why us?" I asked pathetically. My eyes were welling.

He shrugged. He looked to Mr. Hall who looked back at him, but made no such denial of understanding.

"She knew Rory was going to Ireland, why would she leave him the house?" I said. I flung my eyes wildly around the room where they were met on all sides by books. "And the books …" *Are filled with money.*

My eyes fell on *The Selkie Folk*, which stuck out at an odd angle from the time I'd cracked it open and had not pushed it back in properly.

… the human part of him will not age until he walks again on two legs … My stomach grew queasy as fragments of the old woman's voice filled my aching head. Mr. Hall was watching me intensely. His eyes were boring into mine. He was willing me to understand something, but I just couldn't quite see what. Or I didn't want to.

I made a movement to get up, to go crack open every last one of those books, but then something occurred to me.

I can watch the rest of the scene in my head as if it was yesterday. I can hover above, near the cracked ceiling, and watch the pieces tumble into place. I was so confused then, down there in that dusty room. From above, it's all so clear. Like a movie.

"Mr. Hall," I say breathlessly. "Where's the other skin?"

Why wasn't Rory at home when Captain Harville called? I think. My hands are trembling and I feel a horror I never knew was possible.

Mr. Hall points to the corner of the room just as I hear footsteps on the stairs outside and someone calls my name. On a chair in the corner is a brownish gray length of material. It looks like the skin of an elephant. I rush to pick it up, running my fingers across it. It smells unmistakably of the ocean. My relief is mixed up with fear and confusion.

"Cora!" He bursts into the room. My Rory. He is not tall, but built strong. Like a swimmer.

"The money—in the books—Cora, you can come visit me! We won't have to wait!"

He was adopted.

"You can come with me and just stay a few months, you can stay forever, you can go to school, we can do whatever! Anything we want!"

He is dark. He is beautiful in an unreal way. His dark hair waves across his forehead in a perfect stroke that makes my knees weak. His skin is tanned and freckled. There are sun spots on his arms. Those arms taught me to swim, they are thick and strong. They are sure in the water.

Ronan. *Little seal.*

TO BE CONTINUED...

Continue the *Hearts Out of Water* series with
Lifespan of a Memory and *The Last Secret*, out now!

ACKNOWLEDGMENTS

This book wouldn't have been possible without a great many people, a few of which include: my mom and dad (who first gave me the writing bug), my brother Mike, my forever dog Princess, my aunts and uncles (who fostered the writing bug), my favorite Rottweiler mix Lucy, my own Irish dream guy, and all the English teachers I ever had.

Special thanks to my beta reader, Jane Cosby, my editor, Randy Cosby, and my brilliant Irish translator, who shall remain nameless because there's a good chance he'll be running for political office some day.

ABOUT THE AUTHOR

A short, dog-obsessed, ketchup-loving romantic from the middle of the U.S., Annie Cosby spent three years living in Galway, Ireland, which gave her mono, set her soul on fire, and introduced her to her husband.

She is the author of the *USA Today*-recommended *Hearts Out of Water* and *Souls Out of Ireland* series, the Amazon-chart-soaring *Humming Song Saga,* and countless other tales seeped in Celtic lore.

She now lives in St. Louis, Missouri, with a Rottweiler mix named Lucy and her favorite Irishman.

Sign up for her Readers Club and find more bookish fun at AnnieCosby.com.

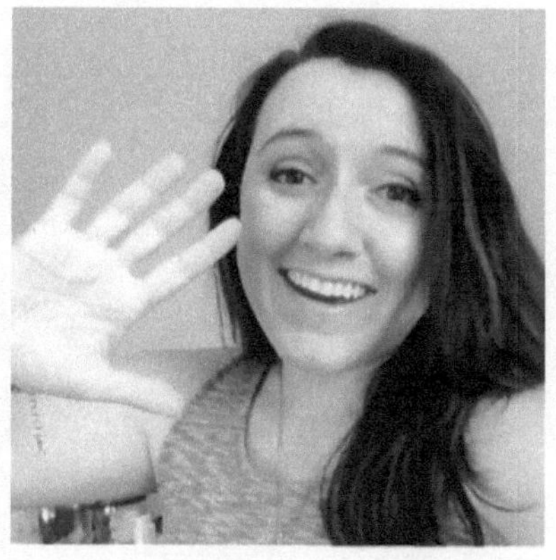

BOOKS BY ANNIE COSBY

HEARTS OUT OF WATER

All the Tales We Tell

Lifespan of a Memory

The Last Secret

Fadó, Fadó: Selkies, Kelpies and Other Celtic Creatures

(A Companion Collection to Hearts Out of Water)

SOULS OUT OF IRELAND

The Daughters of Morrigan

THE HUMMING SONG SAGA

Daughter of the Diamond King